"You're an inspiration, Micah…"

"No, not even close. Someone reached out and gave me a hand up. I want to do the same for others. Everyone deserves that."

"But your compassion helps change lives. That's evident by what you're doing here." Paige shrugged. "Who knows? Maybe God allowed you to go through everything you did so you'd be in a place to help someone else."

Micah laughed, the tone a bit raw and ragged. "Seems ironic that I had to lose an arm to give a hand up to others."

"I'm sorry for everything you've gone through." Paige reached for Micah's hand and gave it a squeeze. "God has a purpose for you. For this house." She tapped his chest. "And it started here. If you didn't care, you wouldn't have come home for Ian's funeral."

And she wouldn't need to guard her heart to keep from falling for Micah.

Because he was right—they needed to stay on track to meet their goals.

And she couldn't lose sight of that by doing something silly…like falling in love.

Heart, home and faith have always been important to **Lisa Jordan**, so writing stories with those elements comes naturally. Happily married for over thirty years to her real-life hero, she and her husband have two grown sons, and they are embracing their new season of grandparenting. Lisa enjoys quality time with her family, reading good books and being creative with friends. Learn more about her and her writing by visiting www.lisajordanbooks.com.

Books by Lisa Jordan

Love Inspired

Visit the Author Profile page at LoveInspired.com.

His Road to
Redemption

Lisa Jordan

LOVE INSPIRED
INSPIRATIONAL ROMANCE

LOVE INSPIRED®
INSPIRATIONAL ROMANCE

Recycling programs
for this product may
not exist in your area.

ISBN-13: 978-1-335-56747-5

His Road to Redemption

Copyright © 2021 by Lisa Jordan

This edition published by arrangement with Harlequin Books S.A.

For questions and comments about the quality of this book, please contact us
at CustomerService@Harlequin.com.

Love Inspired
22 Adelaide St. West, 40th Floor
Toronto, Ontario M5H 4E3, Canada
www.LoveInspired.com

Printed in U.S.A.

And we know that all things work together for good to them that love God, to them who are the called according to his purpose.
—*Romans* 8:28

Thank you to the servicemen and women
who sacrifice daily for our freedoms.

Acknowledgments

Most important, thank You, Lord,
for Your amazing grace and redeeming me
so I can tell my story to reflect Your glory.

My family—Patrick, Mitchell, Scott, Sarah
and Bridget. I love you forever.

Special thanks to Tesla Pollen, Dalyn Weller
and Marc and Cindy Briggs for your willingness
to answer my research questions.
Any mistakes are mine.

To my craft partner, Jeanne Takenaka, for
always making time for brainstorming with me.
So blessed by you.

My MBT Masterminds, WiWee sisters,
Joy Seekers Huddle, Coffee Girls, Cyber Sisters,
WWC family—your prayers and encouragement
keep me going…and growing. I love you all.

Melissa Endlich—thank you for continually
encouraging and inspiring me to grow as a
writer. To the Love Inspired team who
works hard to bring my books to print.

Chapter One

Paige had never expected *someday* to happen so quickly.

Especially since her conversation with Ian had taken place less than a month ago.

Now he was gone, and the promise he'd made was in word only.

No one had anticipated her elderly neighbor and friend's "just a little cold" would develop into pneumonia right before Christmas and cause him to pass away less than two weeks later.

She'd never expected to ring in the New Year by attending his funeral, either.

Still wearing her long-sleeved royal blue A-line dress with a black belt and trim, black riding boots, and her long black wool coat, Paige sat on the rough bench inside the goat barn with

Lulu, one of the pygmy goats, in her lap and stroked the tiny animal's tan and white fur.

Bone-chilling January winds swirled across the snow-laden fields between Ian's property and the Holland dairy farm. Bloated gray clouds blotted out what was left of the afternoon sun, casting her in shadows as they moved across the darkening sky. A shiver slid down the back of her neck despite the pink knitted cashmere scarf looped loosely around her neck.

Pressure mounted behind her eyes, but she blinked back the tears for the hundredth time in the last hour. She hadn't cried when she found Ian collapsed on his kitchen floor. She hadn't cried when they received the news about his passing. She hadn't cried at his funeral that morning. And she wasn't about to break down thirty minutes before she met with his lawyer.

She needed to keep her composure to prove to Ginny Sommers, Ian's attorney, that she was the right person to buy Ian's farm. The farm he had promised to her.

The promise with no proof behind it. Her word against a deceased man's.

She toyed with the silver heart necklace she'd worn daily for the past fifteen years—a nervous habit she hadn't been able to break.

Through the open barn door, she scanned the hillside pasture of the Wilder Goat Farm, where half a dozen Nubian goats browsed on scrubby shrubs sticking up from the snow. Another half dozen Saanens lay on a three-sided climbing platform covered in hay bedding. Three Nigerian dwarf goats chased one another over snow-covered stacks of large, flat rocks.

Located between the Hollands' and her grandparents' properties, Ian's farm had been her sanctuary for as long as she could remember. With Ian and his late wife, Betsy, being best friends with her grandparents, it had become a second home. Now she couldn't stand the thought of it going to some stranger who wouldn't appreciate it the way she did.

Her phone vibrated in her coat pocket. She pulled it out to find a group text with her two best friends, Natalie Bishop and Willow Jennings.

Natalie: You disappeared. Where are you?

Paige: At Ian's farm. Meeting Ginny in 30.

Willow: Praying for you.

Paige: Thanks. I'll let you know how it goes.

Paige stowed her phone as a salt-spattered black SUV pulled into the driveway in front of Ian's farmhouse. She'd expected to see Ginny's silver convertible, but maybe she decided to drive her husband's vehicle due to the inclement weather.

Moving Lulu off her lap, Paige stood and

brushed goat hair off the front of her dress. She probably smelled like the barn, but she really didn't care. She preferred wearing jeans and T-shirts or her usual scrubs over getting dressed up anyway.

Latching the rickety gate behind her, Paige pulled in a deep breath and exhaled slowly, her breath visible in front of her mouth. She pressed a hand against her churning stomach. Hopefully, she appeared more confident than she felt.

When Ginny had called yesterday, asking if they could meet at Ian's house after the funeral, Paige had spent the rest of the evening making sure her business plan was in order.

Dr. Abe O'Brien, the owner and director of the OT clinic in town, had closed his occupational therapy center last month and retired to Florida, putting her out of a job except for the clients she contracted through the local pediatric practice and continued to visit in their homes. Even though he'd given her a generous severance, she couldn't live off it forever.

Natalie and Willow had encouraged her to start the animal-assisted occupational therapy practice she'd been dreaming about doing since she graduated with her master's degree nearly five years ago.

The same dream she'd shared with Ian after she learned of Abe's retirement.

Ian had encouraged that dream by promising her she'd be able to purchase some of his smaller, gentler goats. And he'd agreed to lease part of his property until she could afford to buy it. After all, he'd said the farm was getting too big for one person anyway. Why not use the land to benefit others?

Paige stared at the house that used to be like a second home. Ian and his wife, Betsy, had become surrogate grandparents for her and her sister. Losing Betsy several years ago had been tough, and now with Ian gone, what was she going to do?

She'd keep busy and honor Ian's—and Betsy's—memory by following through with the plans she'd shared with him.

That was going to be her argument to convince Ginny to sell the property to her.

After stopping by her car to retrieve her computer bag, Paige slung the strap over her shoulder and hurried across the barnyard. She slowed her steps as she reached Ian's side yard, which was covered in about four inches of snow. No need to look like she was in a hurry.

Instead of trudging through the snow, she diverted to the road and walked to the driveway. She didn't see Ginny's slim figure dressed in her usual business suit. Instead, a man exited the vehicle wearing a black suit, the right sleeve hanging empty at his side. Dark, wavy hair brushed his collar.

He didn't need to turn around to identify himself.

Micah Holland.

The prodigal son had finally come home.

Paige's heart sank. She steeled her spine and lifted her chin. Just as she has done most of her life around him.

As if sensing her presence, he turned and slipped off dark sunglasses. His eyes widened, then he scowled. He thrust his left hand in the front pocket of his trousers. "Paige? What are you doing here?"

She waved her hand toward the barn. "I was tending to the goats."

"Dressed like that?" His eyes scanned over her.

She glanced down at her clothes. "What's wrong with the way I'm dressed?"

"Everything. I mean, nothing." He ground his jaw, then held up a hand. "Let me start again. You look great. But you're in a dress and boots. Not exactly appropriate attire for chores."

Huh. Micah thought she looked great. First compliment he'd given her. Ever.

She lifted a shoulder. "I wasn't really doing chores right now anyway. After the funeral, I just… I guess I just needed to get away. And this was the first place I could think of."

He nodded, and his jaw tightened. He swallowed a couple of times. "Yeah, I hear you."

"What about you? Taking a trip down memory lane?"

He dragged his hand through inky-black hair long overdue for a cut. His trimmed beard covered most of his chin except for the faded, puckered burn scars on the right side of his jaw and neck where the hair couldn't grow.

Despite the lines of fatigue ringing his eyes, he looked…good. Very good.

"I'm meeting with Ginny Sommers, Ian's lawyer, in about—" he looked at his watch "—twenty minutes. I'm early, but I thought… I don't know…" His voice trailed off.

Yeah, she got it.

Stamping her feet to warm her frozen toes, she shoved her chilled hands in her pockets and wrapped her fingers around her cell phone. "I have a meeting with Ginny in about twenty minutes, too."

"Why would we have appointments at the same time?"

"I have no idea. But I had hoped to talk with Ginny privately."

"Why?"

"Why does it matter to you?" She winced

as soon as the snarky words left her mouth. "Sorry."

"Whatever, Paige." His eyes had lost their spark as he turned away from her and moved to the edge of the driveway, his attention focused toward the barn.

Where were the wisecracks? The insults? The put-downs she'd heard so much growing up down the road from him.

How was she supposed to talk to this stoic person?

Having known Micah since elementary school, Paige had always thought of him as a goofball. Someone who showed off to get the other kids to laugh. The one who waited until the last minute to turn in assignments. Which drove her crazy when they worked together on group projects. And despite his inability to open books, Micah ended up on the honor roll every marking period. The class clown had also beat her out for valedictorian at the end of their senior year. Despite the hours she put in studying and the sacrifices she'd made, she'd always come in second to Micah. She'd never been number one.

At Ian's funeral, he'd sat apart from others, staying on the fringes of the crowd. Even with his own family.

The easygoing all-around guy was gone. In

his place stood a man who had seen the worst and come out scarred and broken.

Even though she had heard he'd been home for brief visits over the past few years, she hadn't seen him since he enlisted in the army.

Had it been eight years already?

She set her computer bag on the edge of the porch, then stood in front of him. "So, how are you doing?"

He laughed, a brittle sound that iced her heart. "Great. Just great. The one guy who believed in me is now gone, and I didn't get to say goodbye."

She longed to wrap her arms around him, knowing that deep need for comfort, but she kept her fists balled in her pockets. "I'm so sorry."

The three words seemed so insignificant, but what else could she say? She understood that pain of not being able to say goodbye. How it shadowed her relationships, especially since she'd lost her father unexpectedly in a traffic accident when she was thirteen.

He shrugged, then turned and looked at her. "It is what it is. Did Ginny tell you anything about this meeting?"

"She called yesterday to ask if we could meet here after the funeral."

"Why here and not her office?"

Paige lifted her hands, palms toward the sky. "I have no idea."

The sound of an approaching vehicle drew their attention to the quiet country road. A silver convertible pulled into the driveway behind Micah's SUV.

"Looks like we're about to find out." Micah moved past her, his empty right sleeve brushing her arm.

Ginny Sommers, Ian's thirtysomething lawyer, stepped out of her car, slipped her expensive sunglasses on top of her head and smiled at them. Wearing a long designer coat and holding on to a leather case, she closed the door. "I know it's not a celebratory day, but Happy New Year." She extended her gloved right hand to Paige, who shook it. Then she turned to Micah, shifted her case from her left to her right, and extended her left hand to him. "Thanks for meeting me."

He shook it. "Ms. Sommers, why here and not your office?"

"Call me Ginny, please. We are here at Ian's request." She jerked her head toward the front door. "Shall we step inside?"

Paige hadn't been inside Ian's house since finding him unconscious before she'd called 911. That wasn't the way she wanted to remember her friend.

She wanted to remember his dry wit, his quiet

prayers and the gentle way he treated his animals. And the truth laced in his words of wisdom.

Her throat thickened as she battled a fresh surge of tears. Releasing a sigh that clouded in front of her, Paige moved past Micah, who held the door, and followed Ginny into the house, bracing herself for the memories that shadowed every room.

She'd listen to what Ginny needed to say. Then, after this joint meeting, she'd set up her own private appointment and show Ginny why she was the best person to buy Ian's farm.

She'd do whatever it took to preserve Ian and Betsy's legacy. She owed them that much.

Micah had wanted to come home in his own time, on his own terms. To prove to his family he was worthy of the Holland name. But one phone call had changed all that.

One life-changing phone call that knocked him to his knees.

And apparently, the hits were still coming.

He rubbed a thumb and forefinger over his gritty eyes, then looked at Ginny and Paige. "So you're saying Ian left the property to both of us?"

Nodding, Ginny folded her hands on the sturdy oak table, scarred from years of use. "Yes, that's exactly what I'm telling you. Around Thanksgiving, Ian came into my office after learning he had an aggressive form of cancer. Due to the size of the tumor on his pancreas and how quickly it had spread to nearby organs, treatments were available to keep him comfortable, but surgery and chemo or radiation weren't options."

"The pneumonia wasn't out of the blue, then? It was related to his cancer?" Paige pushed away from the table, wrapped her arms around her waist and moved to the kitchen sink, where she stood with her back to them. "Why didn't he say anything?"

"From what I understand, yes, the pneumonia was a complication brought on by the cancer. I encouraged Ian to tell people he was sick, but he chose to handle it on his own. As his attorney, I needed to honor his desire for confidentiality. With his wife, Betsy, gone and no children of their own, Ian was ready to leave this earth. But he wanted his property to go to the ones he felt would appreciate it and could benefit the most from it—you two."

After loosening his tie and unbuttoning the top button on his shirt, Micah leaned back in the chair missing a spindle and stretched out his right leg, hoping to ease some of the tightness from the damaged limb. He'd done too much sitting already today. He needed to walk. To think.

"How's this going to work? We divide everything fifty-fifty?"

"That's a great question, and I'm glad you asked. Ian was very clear on the division of property." Ginny retrieved another stack of papers from her leather briefcase. "Micah, you are to receive the house, the pond and a portion of the land that edges your family's dairy farm. And, Paige, you're to receive the goats, the pasture, the barns and the land that borders your grandparents' property."

Micah opened his mouth, but Ginny held up a hand. "Before you speak, Micah, I'd like to get through this next section, because I believe it's quite important."

Paige turned away from the sink and returned to the chair next to Micah, shooting him a look he couldn't quite decipher.

Yeah, he wasn't happy about the arrangement, either.

Ginny turned two papers toward them and used a pen as a pointer. "Paige, according to Ian, you two had a conversation recently where he promised you the goats should you choose to follow through with your desire to open an animal-assisted occupational therapy program. He was always so grateful for the way you helped with Betsy after her stroke and felt you were the most compassionate therapist she had."

Paige blinked rapidly. "Betsy was my grandma's best friend, and she was one of the kindest people I knew. Caring for her was a blessing."

"Well, Ian greatly appreciated everything you did for him. By giving you the goats, the barns and a section of the property, he wanted to see your therapy work flourish."

Paige picked up the paper in front of her and skimmed it. Her hand flew to her mouth as she shook her head. "I don't know what to say."

Ginny turned to Micah. "Ian wanted you to have the house because he said the two of you talked about wanting to help homeless veterans, correct?"

"Yes, but that was a while ago. I'm surprised he remembered."

"Ian was one of the sharpest men I've known. And he understands what it's like to be offered a second chance. By leaving you the house, the pond and a parcel of land, maybe you can carry on his legacy of offering second chances by helping others."

Micah reached for the paper Ginny pushed toward him, but the words blurred on the page. If it hadn't been for Ian, Micah wasn't sure which direction his life would've taken. It hadn't been heading in the right one, that was for sure.

A single middle-of-the-night phone call to Ian nearly six months ago, asking for bail money, had come with conditions—Ian was offering a one-and-done deal. Micah needed to shut down his pity party and turn his life around by making better choices or Ian wouldn't answer his phone the next time.

After all, his family had dealt with enough heartache after the tornado swept across Holland Hill eight years ago, killing Micah's mother and nearly destroying the family farm—they didn't need to lose a son and brother on top of everything else they'd gone through.

Micah cleared his throat and forced his emotions under control. "So that's it, then? Do we have to sign paperwork?"

Ginny clicked her pen a few times, then shuffled through more papers. "Not quite. This inheritance comes with a couple of conditions."

Of course. With Ian, nothing was ever easy.

"Although the roofs are new, Ian knew the house and barn were going to need repairs, especially when you will have to factor in meeting state codes and regulations. In addition to the property you're receiving, Ian left each of you one hundred thousand dollars to invest in your programs."

Micah's eyes widened, and he shot a glance at Paige. Her jaw dropped open like a smallmouth bass.

While he'd forgo all of it in a second to have

Ian back, maybe returning home wasn't going to be so bad after all.

With Ian's help, Micah could get his transitional home and peer-to-peer program set up and finally prove to his family he was no longer Micah the Menace or the runt always struggling to catch up to his older, more successful brothers.

He could tie into the family's Fatigues to Farming program and show he wasn't reckless and irresponsible. While their program taught disabled veterans farming skills to set up their own small businesses—and he admired their intentions—his family didn't understand the physical and mental struggles that came with becoming disabled.

But he did.

Losing a limb did that to a man.

Micah rubbed the phantom pain in his right shoulder where his arm had been blown off four years ago.

And now, with Ian's help, Micah could offer a hand up to some of his veteran brothers to give them that hope they desperately needed to claim a second chance at living a successful life.

A second chance that had been given to him.

As much as Micah loved his childhood neighbor and mentor, Ian didn't give things freely. He lived by the proverb "If you give a man a fish, you feed him for a meal. If you teach a man to fish, you feed him for a lifetime."

Ian had taught many to fish. Including him.

Micah glanced at Paige, then focused on Ginny. "So, what's the catch?"

Smiling, Ginny pulled out two envelopes and tapped them against her palm. "You knew Ian well, didn't you? While Ian believed in both of you and your dreams, he also believed the two of you would be better together."

"Right." Paige scoffed. "Maybe Ian wasn't as sharp as you thought he was."

Micah raised an eyebrow at her. "Paige and I haven't seen each other in years. How does Ian think we could be better together now?"

"You both bring wonderful skill sets to the table. Paige, as I've mentioned already, Ian felt you were one of the best therapists he knew. And Micah—Ian always appreciated your ability to listen and show compassion to someone going through a difficult time. You understand the struggles that veterans like yourself have endured. While you're both creating two completely different programs, he felt you could combine them in some way for the greater good."

"Greater good? What does that mean? While I appreciate Ian's confidence in me—" Paige waved a finger between her and Micah "—in us, I don't see how homeless veterans and children with disabilities can coexist in the same program. I have to ensure my clients are safe at all times."

Micah slid his chair back and pushed to his feet. Dragging his hand over his face, he paced in front of the sink. "Just because someone is homeless, that doesn't mean they are harmful, Paige."

She clutched the silver heart hanging around her neck. "I understand that, Micah. I'm just saying, Ian may have been a bit misguided in his thinking. Anyone working in my program will need to have clearances. Studies have shown that many people who are homeless also struggle with mental illness. Plus, a percentage of them have committed a crime or have been incarcerated."

Ginny held up a hand. "Let me put your minds at ease. Ian was quite clear and focused during our conversation. I had no reason to believe he wasn't in a sound state of mind. I believe Ian saw something in you two that you don't see in yourselves or maybe in each other. By working together, he felt you will be able to bring out the best in one another and create programs that will be beneficial to the community. Both of you will receive the money in three installments. Upon signing paperwork today, you will receive a check for twenty-five thousand dollars to get you started. Then you will have thirty days to meet your next milestone, which will include producing a business plan, working up a budget and meeting with an architect or contractor of your choosing. Once your adviser signs your paperwork, you'll receive another check for twenty-five thousand dollars. Then, once you complete the final milestone, which will show steps toward remodeling your properties and marketing your future programs, you'll receive a final check for fifty thousand dollars."

Micah held up a hand. "Whoa, wait a minute. There's a deadline? We have goals to complete? And who are our advisers? This sounds like a lot of hassle. Why would Ian do this?"

Paige raised an eyebrow. "What's the matter, Micah? Afraid you might have to follow through on something?"

Micah flicked his eyes to Paige. "Listen, lady, you don't know anything about me anymore, so keep your opinions to yourself."

He regretted his sharp tone the moment Paige lowered her head. Scarlet stained her cheeks as she curled the edge of the paper around her fingers.

Yeah, working with her was going to be just peachy.

Micah blew out a breath and gripped the edge

of the sink. "What if we decide not to work together?"

"If either of you decides to walk away from this arrangement, then you will retain your inherited properties and the twenty-five grand, but neither one of you will receive the rest of the money, and it will be donated to the programs Ian chose as a backup."

Paige jerked a thumb at him. "So if he bails, then I lose out? That's not fair."

Ginny lifted her shoulders and held out her hands. "With it being Ian's money, I guess he could make up any conditions he wanted."

"Is that legal?"

Ginny shot him a look, and he realized the stupidity of his own question. Of course it was legal, considering an attorney was overseeing his will.

"Ian wrote letters to each of you, explaining what and why he did it this way. You don't have to sign today if you'd like to take the rest of the weekend to think things through. I understand it's a large undertaking. Talk with one another and come up with a plan on how you will combine your programs. Once you do sign the paperwork, however, you will have sixty days to get your programs in place."

Paige fingered the heart on her silver necklace once again. "Sixty days? That's not possible—

it will probably take longer than that to get appointments for some of the inspections I'd need."

"I understand that. The purpose isn't to have your programs up and running but to be moving forward with your goals."

A band tightened around Micah's head, creating a dull ache at the back of his skull. Ian was demanding the impossible.

Ginny stood and gathered her papers, tapping them on the table to straighten them before putting them back in her case. "Let's meet in my office on Monday. You can share your plans, then we can move forward with the next steps. How does that sound?"

"Ludicrous. Impossible. Ridiculous. Need I go on?"

Ginny pressed a gentle hand on his arm. "Micah, I understand it's a lot to take in. You do not have to agree with this. You will still receive the house and the check for twenty-five thousand. But if you choose to walk away, then Paige doesn't receive the rest of her money, either."

Micah wanted to punch something. The last four years had been nothing short of a living nightmare, and for a brief moment, he'd hoped he'd been cut a break.

But apparently not.

A quick glance at Paige and her pleading

eyes reminded Micah, once again, this wasn't just about him. He had more than himself to consider. Not only did this affect Paige and her clients, but also the veterans who needed help. Help Ian was enabling him to give.

Despite the way Paige had always managed to get under his skin with her hypercompetitive nature while they were growing up, they weren't children any longer. He couldn't walk away, no matter how much he wanted to. It was time to man up, dig in and do the work. No matter how overwhelming it felt.

Once again, Ian was giving him a hand up, and Micah wasn't going to let him down.

Chapter Two

❧

Growing up down the road from the eccentric goat farmer, Paige had always loved Ian's sense of humor, but this was going too far. How was she supposed to get a program in place in sixty days?

And work with Micah Holland?

No way.

At least, not without one—or maybe even both—of them walking away with another scar or two.

Maybe he'd consider letting her buy him out.

Needing some time to sort through the million different thoughts tumbling through her head, Paige walked out of Ian's house with Ginny. Once the attorney pulled out of the driveway and headed down the road, Paige returned to her car parked in the barnyard. She dropped her computer bag on the passenger seat, then headed for the barn.

No need to set up a separate meeting—Ian had given her what she wanted. Mostly, anyway. But now it came with a price.

She opened the gate to the pen, taking note of one of the hinges coming loose from the weathered wood.

Might as well start making a list now that she was going to own the place.

The goats bleated and came running. She checked their feed and refilled their water. If she'd been dressed in jeans and a sweatshirt, she would have dropped to the cold straw-covered runway between the stalls and allowed them to climb on her. But still wearing the blue dress from the funeral, she sat once again on the wooden bench near the barn door, which was stripped to gray from years of exposure to the elements.

She didn't really care if the dress got snagged on the weathered wood, because she wouldn't be wearing it again. Not when it carried so many painful memories.

Ian's death had affected more people than he probably would've realized.

Lulu ran over to her.

Paige picked up the small animal and held

her on her lap like she did her French bulldog, Charlotte.

She ran a hand over Lulu's back while scanning the property. Not only would Ian's house need extensive work inside to make it accessible, but the tan exterior needed a fresh coat of paint. A break in the clouds allowed a sliver of sunlight to shine on the hunter-green metal roof on the house. The backyard needed a good landscaper once the snow melted to restore the gardens Betsy had spent years cultivating.

But that wasn't Paige's problem—that was up to Micah to take care of now. She needed to focus on the barns and her own property.

How was she going to get a therapy center built in the middle of winter? No contractor wanted to work in brain-numbing temperatures.

But somehow Paige needed to make this work.

Her clients depended on her.

Her family depended on her.

Letting them down wasn't an option.

Setting Lulu on the floor, Paige stood and flipped on the light. Her eyes roamed over the rustic interior of the barn, taking in the water-stained wood and beams of light streaming between the cracks in walls. A couple of worn wires showed that getting the electric updated needed to be a priority.

Winding her scarf tighter around her throat,

turning up her collar to ward off a chill and buttoning her coat, Paige headed outside. She rounded the back side of the goat barn, making note of rotted boards that needed to be replaced.

At least the pole barn was brand-new—the tan metal structure with a hunter-green metal roof that matched the house had been built at the end of the summer to hold a couple of antique tractors Ian had wanted to buy.

But it remained empty.

Instead of purchasing the tractors, Ian had started selling off some of his herd in the early fall, dairy goats followed by meat goats.

Now she knew why.

Ian, why didn't you say something about being sick?

"Hey!"

Paige's head jerked up. Still dressed in his suit, Micah strode across the yard with a black-and-white pygmy goat tucked against his chest. Deep impressions in the snow showed his path from the pond to the barn.

She rushed out of the gate, taking the wayward animal from him. "Daffy, what are you doing out of your pen?"

"I found her by the pond behind the house."

Paige sighed. "Sorry about that. I don't know how she could've gotten out."

"Hole in the fence, maybe?"

"If so, then it's recent. Ian and I did a perimeter check about a month ago. Right before he got sick." Even mentioning his name caused her throat to tighten. But she didn't have time for tears, especially in front of someone else.

As she opened the gate to set Daffy inside, Rosie, her twin, raced past her legs and darted toward the road. Thankfully, Micah was outside the fence and scooped up the second runaway. He placed her back inside, then brushed his hand against his pant leg. "Let's check the fence again and do a makeshift repair to keep these little escapees confined."

They walked the perimeter, looking for the smallest holes in the welded wire where the goats could have pushed against the fence too much and created sags or even holes where the wire separated.

Near the back side of the barn, they found a spot where the fence had come apart, giving the smaller goats a large enough space to climb in and out at will.

Micah pulled his phone out of his pocket. "I'll call the farmhouse and see if anyone is around to give us a hand with repairing this fencing."

Paige fisted a hand on her hip. "Put your phone away. Even though I'm a woman, I can repair fencing."

A quick smile flashed across Micah's face,

chasing away the deep lines in his forehead and the fatigue around his eyes. For a second, she was transported back a decade, when life wasn't as challenging…for him, at least.

"This has nothing to do with your gender, but more with your career choice. You're a therapist, not a farmer."

"Well, apparently, I'm about to be both. Besides, I've been around this farm most of my life. I know how to fix this. Ian was a great teacher. There's a roll of fencing in the barn. I can weave a section in place until I replace the whole thing."

"You're not exactly dressed for wire repair." His eyes skimmed over her blue dress.

"Maybe so, but the fence needs to be fixed today to ensure the animals' safety." Without waiting for a rebuttal, Paige strode back to the barn, found the roll of woven wire, a pair of gloves, wire cutters, ties and a spool of high-tensile wire. Careful not to snag her dress, she carried everything out of the barn and found Micah waiting near the gate. Without asking, he took the roll of woven wire from her, hoisted it onto his shoulder and carried it around back to the damaged area.

After slipping on Ian's too-large leather gloves, she unrolled the wire. Micah held it in place while she took the ends and wrapped them around the existing wire, creating a hinge point to secure it in place so she could pull the roll to cover the damaged area.

"How's your family doing?" Micah asked as they worked.

She eyed him, but he kept his gaze focused on what she was doing. She'd figured he'd bring up the bombshell Ginny just dropped on him. But maybe, like her, he needed time to process. So small talk could fill the awkward silence between them.

"They're doing well. Grandpa retired from preaching about five years ago. They usually spend a couple of months in Florida, but when Ian got sick, they decided to stay put for the time being. Mom's still the adult librarian at the Shelby Lake Public Library. Abby graduated high school last June, and now she has a daily caregiver who comes in while Mom works. She takes Abby shopping. They work on weekly goals, bake and visit different places in the community. Plus, she has a physical therapist who works with her a couple of times a week, and then I help Mom with her in the evenings."

Paige secured the wire to the fence posts with the T-post ties and used the high-tensile wire to sew the two fence sections together at the top, the bottom and across the damaged area, pulling the fence in tight to prevent future escapes.

"She's why you became an OT, right? Because of her CP?"

Paige nodded. "When we were kids, I saw how much her therapists helped her thrive and decided I wanted to do the same." She knew Micah was aware of Abby's spastic diplegia, a form of cerebral palsy that affected her hips and legs, and appreciated his interest. "She's been using her wheelchair more and more now, but she doesn't let it get her down."

"I'm sorry to hear that. I'll have to stop by and see her sometime. Does she still love music?"

"She'd love to see you. And yes, she does." Paige flashed him a smile and took a step back, dropping the backs of her hands on her hips. "It's not pretty, but it will hold until I can get the fence replaced."

Micah still held the spool of high-tensile wire. "Is there anything you can't do?"

She looked at him, ready to shoot off a retort, but he looked at her with…admiration? Was he actually being sincere?

Huh.

Two compliments in one day?

She shrugged. "I had to rely on myself and learn how to figure things out on my own after Dad passed away. Mom was working or caring for Abby. My grandparents were busy with their ministry. Like I said—Ian was a great teacher.

Patient and kind. What he didn't show me, I've learned by reading and watching online videos."

"You're going to be a formidable opponent, Paige Watson."

"Opponent? Why is everything a competition with you?"

Micah frowned. "Me? You're the one who had to prove you were the best person for the award, the job, the whatever."

She yanked the gloves off, then smacked them on the fence post. "I had to work hard and earn everything I've achieved. I couldn't run off and join the military when life became too difficult to deal with."

Micah clenched his jaw. "Yeah, being blamed for causing my mother's death, then nearly getting my team killed and losing an arm in the process was such a piece of cake. Shame on me for taking the easy way out."

Heat scalded her face for the second time in an hour as Micah set the spool of wire on the fence post, then turned and strode across the yard. A moment later, his SUV door slammed and he peeled out of the driveway.

Way to go, Paige.

She buried her face in her grimy hands. Why did she let him get under her skin like that? She'd never talk to anyone else that way, so why did she have to be so snarky with him?

With the wind chafing her cheeks and feeling the emotional weight of the day pressing on her, Paige slipped back inside the pen. She reached for the gloves only to find one missing. Lulu headed toward the back of the pen with the other glove in her mouth.

Little scavenger.

Paige chased after her, retrieved the glove, then gathered the rest of the fencing supplies and stowed them back in the barn. Once she made sure again the animals had enough food and water, she left the pen, secured the gate and headed for her car.

After backing out of the driveway, Paige drove in the other direction toward her grandparents' house.

How were she and Micah going to survive working together if ten minutes in each other's company had one of them walking away?

Somehow they were going to have to figure out a plan—and sooner rather than later—because she had clients depending on her, and she couldn't let them down.

But first she needed to apologize. Whatever his intentions had been, he'd suffered greatly. She needed to show Micah she was on his side. And that they could be partners, because after all, they just wanted what was best for others.

* * *

What was Ian thinking, forcing him to work with Paige?

With her last comment still echoing inside his head, Micah slammed the driver's side door and strode into Ian's house. After changing into worn jeans and a navy sweatshirt and shrugging into his leather jacket, the growling in his stomach became a distraction. He needed food and some medicine for the ache in his right leg.

And a plan.

Even though he wanted nothing more than to quit and walk away, he couldn't.

Unfortunately, what needed to be done to make the house habitable for his veteran buddies was much greater than he had expected.

Before she left, Ginny had given him the house keys and told him to make himself at home.

Easier said than done without Ian puttering around the old place.

But it may have been the reprieve Micah needed. Even though he loved his family, he wasn't ready to spend the evening in the controlled chaos of having his niece and nephews running around. They just reminded him of what he'd never have—a family of his own.

First, he had to find someone willing to look past his scars to get to know his heart.

And right now, that seemed like a long shot.

Micah headed into the kitchen. Even though he hadn't spent much time at Ian's place since he'd enlisted, the room had remained the same as Betsy had left it before she passed, including the outdated calendar of goats hanging on the faded floral-papered wall. Worn dark cabinets that Ian had built needed a good cleaning to remove the layers of accumulated grease, chipped almond-colored appliances needed replacing, and brown-and-white patterned floor tile lifting in corners appeared as tattered as Micah felt.

But the place was clean and it had good bones. Even though Ian had spent the past couple of weeks in the hospital, he had a lady who came in to clean and keep his kitchen stocked.

Still, despite the full fridge and freezer, Micah wasn't in the mood to cook. Without his adaptive equipment, it would take even longer to get something to eat. Maybe he'd drive down the hill and grab a burger from Joe's Diner.

Micah stepped out onto the front porch and zipped his jacket against the chill icing his neck. A gray sedan pulled in behind his SUV.

Paige stepped out of the car and slammed the door. Still wearing her dress from the funeral, she drew her coat tighter around her and strode to the porch, head bent against the wind.

"Paige. What are you doing here? Have more life advice for me?"

She rested a gloved hand on the railing and looked up at him, a shadow passing over her blue eyes. "I owe you an apology. I'm sorry for what I said. I didn't mean to disrespect you that way. I'd like to think we can work well together, and the sooner we come up with a plan, the quicker we can meet our goals."

His eyes tangled with hers, taking in her auburn hair falling in waves around her shoulders. Winter cold reddened the tip of her nose, which was covered in a light sprinkle of freckles. Then he nodded and reached for the front door. He stepped back and waited for her to walk ahead of him into the house. "Let's talk inside where it's warmer."

His stomach would have to wait, because Paige was right.

Heavy darkening clouds lumbered across the sky, chasing away the remnants of sunshine. A storm was coming.

In more ways than one.

Closing the door firmly behind him, Micah entered Ian's foyer after Paige, getting slapped in the face by years of memories once again.

If he closed his eyes and concentrated, he could hear Ian's laughter and his deep bass voice as he sang along with the country station on the radio.

"Would you like something to drink?"

"Water's fine."

Micah strode into the kitchen, shrugged out of his jacket and draped it over a chair, then opened the fridge. He pulled out two bottles of water, set one in front of her, then shut the door with his shoulder.

Holding the bottle between the counter and his waist, Micah uncapped it, then took a long drink, draining half the liquid. He set it on the counter, then turned to Paige. "I've had enough sitting for one morning. Let's walk through the house, then we can tour the property. Unless you'd rather wait until you're dressed a little warmer."

"Now's fine." Still wearing her coat with the collar flipped up to guard her neck, she shook her head, grabbed her bottle and followed him.

They moved into the living room, where the sight of Ian's empty recliner punched Micah in the chest. He crossed to the window and opened the curtains, exposing a view of the backyard and the pond covered in a layer of ice.

The living room, with its large bay window, wooden floor in need of a shine and shabby furniture, had been Ian and Betsy's favorite place in the house. Even after Betsy passed, Ian hadn't allowed anyone to move her favorite chair that offered the best view for watching the ducks on the water.

Paige moved to the window, took a drink of her water and then wrapped her arms around her waist. "What did Ginny mean by you wanting to help homeless veterans?"

"After I separated from the army, I got involved in a ministry run by Ian's brother, Phil—the Next Step, which is a transitional home that helps homeless veterans shift back into society with secure jobs and permanent housing. Phil's place in Pittsburgh has enough space for ten guys. He offers room and board in exchange for help around the house. The men meet monthly with a counselor, attend church and create weekly goals, even if they're small ones. They're also required to have jobs. For the first year, they reestablish the skills they need for a successful life. Most men leave the Next Step after a year, but some stay a little longer."

"Sounds like a great program."

He didn't mind sharing about Phil's ministry, and he sensed Paige needed more information to feel comfortable about their pending partnership.

"Yeah, it is. Phil's a lot like Ian, so it felt a little like home. I know what it's like to figure out how to find some sort of semblance of a normal life. Getting these guys off the streets and giving them a sense of hope is one of the first steps. I talked with Phil and Ian about starting a transitional home somewhere in Shelby Lake where guys could escape the bustle of the city and soak in the country setting. My program will be called A Hand Up, because that's what Ian and Phil had given me."

"I really admire your compassion and desire to help these men."

"I just want to pay it forward." He waved his hand across the backyard. "I can offer that here now that Ian's given me the opportunity, and I won't let him down." Micah looked at her, taking in her auburn hair hanging in light waves around her face. "Or you. You can count on me, Paige."

She looked at Micah, then dropped her eyes to her water bottle. "I hope so."

"You don't trust me." Not that he blamed her after the way he just left all those years ago.

Paige shook her head. "It's not that. It's just… I'm not used to relying on others. I work better on my own. Your program is a good thing. A great thing. And I'll do what I can to help you achieve your goal."

"I'd like to partner with my family's Fatigues to Farming program in some way, but my brother Jake and I have been like oil and water since we were kids. He still thinks of me as Micah the Menace."

"I thought the Fatigues to Farming program was set up already to help veterans with disabilities."

"It is, but the veterans who have started that program have a decent support system, whereas the guys who would be moving in here don't have anyone. No one understands a disability like someone who has walked that same road." He lifted his shoulder where his sleeve hung limp at his side. "Beyond the physical, there are emotional and mental hurdles to overcome. I can help them overcome those."

"I don't doubt that, Micah. When you put your mind to something, you see it through. But what about trained professionals such as physical therapists, occupational therapists, counselors, pastors…"

He laughed, the sound echoing off the walls. "I didn't mean I was handling it all on my own. Losing an arm has taught me about the importance of asking for help. No one can do everything on their own. And we weren't meant to. God created us for relationships—with Him and with others. It took me a long time to realize the importance of that. We will have the right resources in place to help the men to thrive."

Paige took another drink of water. "Apparently you've learned more than me over the past several years, because I still find asking for help nearly impossible."

"If you want to make your program a success, then that is one lesson you will need to learn. No matter how painful it may be."

Paige turned away from the window and walked past the bulging bookcases filled with Bibles, Western novels and books on raising goats. She stopped in front of the corner fireplace made of rocks gathered from Arrowhead Creek, which ran through Ian's property. "Micah, I can help you get this house set up with adaptive equipment. The house will need a lot of work to meet ADA guidelines. If you want, I can go with you when you meet with your contractor. For example, instead of having your dishes stacked in cabinets that are eye level, you may want to consider bottom drawers with storage dividers to promote autonomy for those who may be in wheelchairs. The ADA has guidelines on designing houses that are accessible for people with disabilities."

"Yeah, my brother Evan mentioned Dad and Jake had to meet specific guidelines when they had the cabins built for their program."

"That's right. They will be a great resource for you. But still, I'll do my best to help you meet the needs of the men entering your program. I'm not afraid to get my hands dirty, so I'll help with scrubbing walls, painting…whatever it takes to get this house to become a certified transitional home. I believe in the value of your program, and I want to do what I can to help you succeed."

He turned and faced her, his eyes searching hers a minute. Then he nodded. "Thank you, Paige. I appreciate it. How can I help you? What's your vision for your program?"

"When my former boss retired, the thought of me leaving Shelby Lake to find a good job stressed my mom and sister, so I want to do what I can to stay local. Currently, I'm contracted through one of Dr. O'Brien's colleagues' pediatric practice, but I want my own center. To embrace my own vision." Paige lifted her hands, then dropped them at her sides. "Problem is, I'm not a farmer. Even though I've inherited a bunch of goats and I know some of the basics, I have no idea what goes into the daily care and maintenance of the herd. Ian took care of the deworming, hoof trimming, breeding schedules, feeding supplements…you name it. You have a lot more farming experience than I do. I'll need people to help with the daily chores, maintenance and caring for the goats. You said your men will be required to hold down jobs, so maybe I can employ a couple of them to help care for the goats and maybe even train them."

"Jake and Dad are the farmers in the family, but I'll do what I can to help. I have no problem helping with chores and helping you set up a system for their care. Ian wasn't much for using a computer, but he used to write out detailed notes. I'm sure his journals are around here somewhere." Micah rubbed a hand over his face, feeling the effects of getting up at the crack of dawn to drive three hours to make it to Ian's funeral on time. "As for the goats—train them how? These are a bunch of gruff city dudes with poor attitudes. Even though they've been honorably discharged, some of them have served time."

"In order for the goats to be used in my program, they need human interaction and affection. Someone to love them, hold them, pet them. The more attention they get, the less aggressive they will be. Your guys could have a big part in the beginning stages of that program. Caring for animals helps people to grow emotionally and mentally, and it gives them a sense of purpose."

"Yeah, okay. I guess that would work. And maybe it would help bridge the gap between our two programs. Plus, once we get up and running, they could help with the chores and maintenance of the animals. You've put a lot of thought into this. Why goats, though?"

"Goats work well as therapy animals, meaning they're more for emotional support and mental well-being. Some of my clients are resistant to try new tasks and meet new goals. Playing with goats in a controlled setting can help them to overcome some of their frustrations. Also, some of the children I work with struggle with typical clinical settings. They've spent most of their young lives in and out of hospitals, so doing therapy creates anxiety. Having my own practice in a natural environment will ease some of those feelings. With their attention focused on the goats, their therapy will feel more like play and less like work. Plus, I'll still be close to home to help Mom with Abby. Getting a therapy center built in the middle of winter is going to be a challenge, though."

"But not impossible. We'll make it happen." Again, he gave her a long look, then he stuck out his hand. "Partner."

She shook it, then returned hers to her coat pockets. "You know, the last time we partnered together, I nearly received a failing grade on our project because you bailed on me, leaving me to complete it on my own."

Micah raised an eyebrow. "If I remember correctly, I bailed because you wouldn't listen to my input. Everything had to be your way. A partnership is a two-way street based on trust and compromise. Besides, I'm no longer the cocky kid from high school. The sooner you realize that, the quicker we can work together. Let's both stop dwelling on the past and focus on what we need to do to offer hope to those in our programs."

Smothering a yawn, Paige nodded and slid her water bottle in her coat pocket. "I need to head back to my grandparents'. I'm already late for dinner. I'll be in touch tomorrow, and we can discuss our next steps."

Micah walked her out of the living room, her words settling like an invisible cloud around him.

What would it be like to work with Paige again? He'd find out soon enough. And hopefully neither of them would walk away from the experience with scars.

Because he had enough as it was.

Chapter Three

Wanting nothing more than a shower, comfy clothes and maybe a mindless rom-com to ease the sadness from her chest, Paige pulled into the driveway, parked behind her mother's red SUV and trudged up the cleared steps.

The door opened before she could put her hand on the knob.

Charlotte, her black-and-white French bulldog, shot outside and danced around the porch at Paige's arrival.

Still wearing the crimson sweater and black skirt she'd worn to the funeral, Paige's mother stood in the doorway, her honey-blond hair pulled back in a low ponytail at her neck. Though she was only fifty, too many lines etched between her eyebrows showed her constant worry. Tilting her head, Mom's tired eyes searched Paige's face, and she opened her arms. "Your dress is covered in mud. What happened?"

Without a word, Paige scooped up Charlotte, buried her face in the dog's neck, then walked into her mother's embrace. She rested her head on her mom's shoulder, feeling nine years old all over again, when safety had reigned before their lives had fallen apart.

Tears pressed against her closed eyelids, but Paige forced them back. She released a sigh and straightened. She had too much work to do and no time to give in to the well of grief filling her chest. "I had to repair part of the fence, where goats had been escaping."

"By yourself? Couldn't you have called for help? Or at least changed first?" Mom guided her into the house and pulled Paige's coat off her shoulders. "Get washed up and join us in the kitchen. You're just in time for dinner."

"I should run back to the cottage and change."

"I'm sure I have something you can borrow." Mom slid an arm around Paige's shoulders and led her into the foyer that smelled of Italian food and homemade bread.

"Abby's been baking again." Paige lifted her nose and inhaled the scents coming from the kitchen. Paige set Charlotte on the floor, and she scampered into the kitchen.

"Your sister will take any opportunity to

make bread. Run upstairs and rummage through my closet to find something to wear."

After washing up, pulling her hair back into a ponytail and changing out of her dress and into her mother's borrowed gray jeans, a coral-colored sweater and wool socks, Paige headed downstairs to the kitchen, where voices drowned out the soft music playing in the background.

Abby, her twenty-year-old sister, loved all kinds of music, so hearing it every day had become a habit.

Her grandparents' newly renovated farmhouse-style kitchen had been remodeled with cream-colored cabinets, stainless steel appliances and gray countertops. Houseplants lined the windowsill above the sink.

Having changed into jeans and a pink sweatshirt, her mom stood at the stove, cutting into a pan of what appeared to be lasagna.

Paige's grandmother, still wearing a stylish emerald-green wrap dress from the funeral, added tongs to the wooden bowl of salad in the middle of the table. She smiled and opened her arms.

Paige walked into her embrace without hesitation and breathed in her familiar lavender scent. Grandpa sliced the loaf of bread fresh from the bread maker and placed the basket next to the salad. Over Grandma's head, he winked at her. "How you doing, love?"

"I'm fine, Grandpa." Paige moved behind him and wrapped her arms around his waist, pressing her cheek against his back. "How are you?"

She wasn't the only one grieving. Her grandfather had laid his best friend to rest.

Without a word, he gave her a brief nod and squeezed her arms lightly. "How did your meeting go?"

"I'll tell you all about it over dinner." Paige turned, placing a hand on her sister's narrow shoulder. She moved Abby's wheelchair away from the table slightly so she could look her in the face that reminded her so much of their father. Taking Abby's small hands in her own, Paige knelt in front of her, brushing her dark hair off her cheek. "The bread smells great, Abbs. You did a wonderful job."

A smile stretched across Abby's face and lit up her periwinkle-blue eyes. "Thanks, sissy. It's a new recipe. I hope you like it."

"I'm sure I will love it."

Abby lifted a hand and pointed a shaky finger toward Paige's face. "You have sad eyes."

Paige pressed a kiss against her sister's knuckles. "It's been a sad day. But now that I'm here with you, I will feel so much better."

"Can we watch *Mary Poppins* after dinner?"

Paige longed to curl up on her own couch with Charlotte tucked against her side and untangle her thoughts from the day. But the eager look on her sister's face had Paige nodding. "I think that's a great idea."

"Time to eat." Mom set the pan of steaming lasagna in the middle of the table and pulled out a chair next to Abby.

Pushing to her feet, Paige wheeled Abby back in place at the table, then took the seat across from her. Grandpa and Grandma sat at either end of the rectangular black walnut table that had been a fixture in the large kitchen for as long as Paige could remember.

They took hands and Grandpa prayed; his words of gratitude in spite of the sadness that hovered over the room seeped into the cracks in Paige's heart. Then they filled their plates, although no one seemed to have much of an appetite.

"So, how'd your meeting with Ginny go, Paige?"

Paige peered at her grandfather over the rim of her glass of ice water. She set it down, folded her hands in her lap, then scanned her family watching her. "It was quite unexpected. Ian left me half of his property and a sizable inheritance."

She proceeded to tell them about Ian's expectations. "So the next couple of months are going to be extremely busy. I need to get a new therapy center built."

Grandpa rubbed his thumb and forefinger across his chin, his eyes intense as if deep in thought. "Instead of building, what about converting the new pole barn into a therapy center? Sadly, Ian got sick before he could buy those antique tractors he wanted, so it's probably still sitting empty." Grandpa finished the last bite of his lasagna, then pushed his plate away. "The pole barn has a poured foundation and electric and water hookups already, but it will need a bunch of interior work done to create the kind of space you want. Since Grandma and I aren't going to Florida for the rest of the winter, I can lend a hand doing some of the renovations."

For the first time all day, Paige gave a genuine smile. "Thanks, Grandpa. I really appreciate it. I hadn't thought about the pole barn. Maybe instead of having a therapy center, I'll have a therapy barn." She looked at her mother. "Just so we're clear—with this unexpected windfall, I won't be leaving the area to look for a new job."

Across the table, Mom's shoulders sagged as her eyes brightened. "You have no idea how much joy that brings me. I know you're old enough to make your own choices, but I dreaded the thought of you moving away."

Paige wasn't fond of it, either. But she wasn't going anywhere. Her family needed her. And she needed them.

She had a feeling the next couple of months were going to challenge her in ways she wouldn't expect. But she'd do whatever it took to get her program up and running. Even if it meant working with Micah Holland.

She had no idea how to handle Micah the grown man when all she'd known was Micah the boy. But something told her it was going to be an interesting venture as she got to know him all over again.

Micah longed to escape.

But he couldn't.

Sunday dinner at the Holland farm was tradition. As natural as breathing. And being a part of the family meant putting aside his own insecurities and showing up to enjoy quality time together, no matter how loud and chaotic it might be.

The last family dinner he'd attended hadn't included two new spouses, a fiancée and a couple of extra nephews. So, yeah, it had been a while.

But he had only himself to blame.

The door had always been open. He was the one who'd stayed away.

This time was going to be different.

He'd stick around, put down roots for the first time since joining the army and do what it took to fit in. Then, maybe once they saw he wasn't going anywhere, they'd be on board with his transitional home and be willing to partner with him.

Until then, Micah had a long road ahead to live up to everyone's expectations.

Failure wasn't an option.

Olivia, his seven-year-old niece, outnumbered by her twin brother, Landon, and six-year-old cousin, Aidan, raced into the kitchen, ran around the table, then zoomed back through the house, her blond ponytail bouncing against her back while the boys chased her. The family dogs barked and ran around the kids' legs, nearly tripping them.

And Micah had thought hiding in the kitchen with the pretense of cleaning up was going to be quieter.

What was left of Claudia's roast pork with cranberry glaze, a spoonful of herbed mashed potatoes and one remaining biscuit sat abandoned on the stove. Micah searched cabinets for storage containers, then he opened the dishwasher and loaded dirty plates on the bottom rack.

While the rest of the family had bumped shoulders trying to get dinner on the table and keep the kids corralled, they'd all dismissed his offers of help, leaving him feeling a little useless.

So the least he could do was handle cleanup. The coffee maker gurgled its final drip as the scent of fresh brew swirled through the air.

Micah dried his hand on a towel, then opened the cabinet and reached for a cup. He filled it to the rim, then pressed his back against the edge of the sink to sip it, allowing the warm liquid to loosen the band of anxiety around his chest.

Through the window over the kitchen table, shards of sunlight slanted through the bare branches of the apple trees, sending long shadows across last night's fresh snow, unmarred by footprints or dog tracks.

He'd rather shrug into his jacket and take a walk in the crisp air. But he needed to learn to stay put even when it felt hard.

Tucker, his second-to-the-oldest brother, walked into the kitchen, the overhead light stripping his dark brown hair to a lighter blond. He lifted his nose. "Do I smell coffee?"

"Just made a fresh pot." Setting his cup on the stove, Micah turned, pulled another mug out of the cabinet, set it on the counter and filled it. He handed it to Tucker. "Here you go."

"Thanks, man." Tucker took a drink, then sighed. He leaned against the counter and looked at Micah over the rim of his mug. "Everything okay? You were quiet at dinner."

"Just taking it all in. The family keeps growing. And so does the noise level." Palming his cup, Micah laughed, but part of him still wanted nothing more than to head back to Ian's and soak in the solitude as the late-afternoon shadows stretched into evening.

"We're blessed, that's for sure." The grin slid easily across Tucker's face, showing just how much his brother enjoyed his second chance at love with Isabella after losing his first wife, Rayne—and the twins' mother—to an unexpected freak allergic reaction.

Would he have that same kind of happiness someday?

Doubtful. Who wanted a man with a scarred, broken body?

Micah set his half-finished cup back on the stove, then moved back to the sink and rinsed the rest of the dishes before loading them into the dishwasher. "Hey, Tuck?"

"Yeah, man. What's up?"

With his eyes fixed on the windowsill, Micah shook his head. "Never mind. Forget it."

Tucker moved behind him and pressed a hand on Micah's shoulder. "Hey, if there's something you wanna talk about, I'm all ears."

No matter what he had going on in his own

life, Tucker always managed to make time for others, always willing to listen. Just like their mother had been.

Micah exhaled, gripped the edge of the sink, then shut off the water and faced his brother. "I'm sorry for not attending the wedding. I really did plan on being there, but something did come up. I wasn't making excuses, you know."

"I know better than anyone how life happens. No worries, man. You're here now. And that's what's important." Tucker thumped him on the back.

"Yeah." Micah loaded glasses one by one on the top rack in the dishwasher.

But would Tuck still feel the same way if he knew the truth about what had kept Micah from celebrating his special day?

Tucker's wife, Isabella, stepped into the kitchen. Her eyes zeroed in on her husband as she stood on tiptoe to brush a kiss across his lips. "Your dad and Claudia mentioned setting up Pictionary in the family room before everyone has to take off."

Perfect. Games were the norm after family dinners. Or so he'd been told. Usually, Micah wouldn't have minded, but even after having to relearn how to write using his left hand, his drawing talent rivaled that of a toddler.

Maybe he could sit this one out and be a spectator.

Now, at that he excelled.

Micah dropped the dishwashing tablet in the dispenser, then started the appliance. With the kitchen clean once again and counters wiped down, there was little else he could do to stall. Maybe he could sneak out the back and no one would notice his absence.

They'd had plenty of practice with him being gone more than being home.

"Thank you for cleaning up. Now come and join us." Claudia, his stepmother, linked her arm through his and guided him out of the kitchen, blocking his last chance of escape.

They headed into the family room, where the noise level increased, and Olivia patted the space next to her on the oversize ottoman while Landon and Aidan dug into a pile of Legos on the floor next to her. "Uncle Micah, sit by me."

The sweet look on her face should've been directed at someone else, because he certainly didn't deserve it. Any of it.

He didn't belong here. What was he thinking?

"Just a minute, Princess." He held up a finger to her, then took in his brothers gathered on the oversize sectional with their arms wrapped around their wives. Dad sat in the recliner with Claudia sitting on the arm, her hand resting on his shoulder. The family dogs curled up in beds in front of the stone fireplace that expelled much needed warmth in the room.

In the corner, the white Christmas tree lights cast a soft glow across the gleaming wooden floor.

Another holiday he'd missed.

Micah blew out a breath, then shoved his hand in his front pocket. "Before we dive into this rousing Holland tradition, I have something to share."

Claudia straightened, and Dad leaned forward, resting his elbows on his knees. "What's up, son?"

"I had a meeting with Ian's attorney yesterday after the funeral."

"With Ginny? How'd that go?"

"Well, a bit unexpected, to tell you the truth." Micah faced the stone fireplace. His eyes roamed across the framed photos of him and his brothers through the years, including Jake's, Tuck's and his boot camp pictures lining the mantel, a photo of Evan holding a kayak paddle in one hand and a trophy in the other, and Dad and Claudia's wedding photo, then he returned his attention back to Dad. "He left his property to Paige Watson and me."

Micah spent the next ten minutes sharing the

details of Ian's will. "So it looks like Paige and I are going to be partners for a while."

With his infant son, Charlie, sleeping against his chest, Micah's oldest brother, Jake, stood and swayed back and forth in front of the bay window. "Great to hear you'll be sticking around for a while, man."

Micah tried to dissect his brother's tone, but the look on Jake's face showed nothing but genuine interest.

Standing next to the Pictionary easel, Evan capped and uncapped one of the markers with his thumb and forefinger. "Why would he leave the goats to Paige and not you? You're the one with the farming experience. What are you planning to do with the house? Live there?"

Shoving his hand in his front pocket, Micah nodded. "Essentially, yes. I'm going to turn it into a transitional home for homeless veterans with disabilities who don't have any other place to go. And Paige plans to use the goats in her animal-assisted therapy practice."

Natalie, Evan's fiancée and one of Paige's best friends, took the marker from him and laid it on the easel tray. "She's been talking about that for a while. I'm so glad she now has the opportunity to get started."

Charlie stiffened and let out a cry. Jake handed the baby to his wife, Tori. "Shelby Lake doesn't really have a homeless population, so how would something like that benefit the community?"

"Even though Shelby Lake isn't affected directly, I will be partnering with Ian's brother, Phil, who runs a homeless ministry in Pittsburgh. If everything works out the way I hope, I'd like to partner with your Fatigues to Farming program eventually in some way."

"What did you have in mind?" Dad raised an eyebrow and glanced at Jake.

Micah turned to him. "I don't have all the details sorted out yet, but I want to be able to offer a safe place to someone who needs a hand up, a second chance at a new life. Then once they've become stable, they could move into the farming program to learn skills that would enable them to get a job or start their own hobby farm or something. I know your first phase went well, and I believe in what you're doing. From what I understand, the veterans live here with their families. The men who will come into a transitional house feel abandoned by their families and their country, so they need to overcome some other challenges first."

Jake laced his fingers behind his neck. "How'd you get involved in Phil's program?"

Now was the moment of truth. Or at least as much as he wanted to share right now. Micah exhaled softly, then lifted his eyes to look at his dad and each of his brothers. "I was one of those veterans."

Jake's eyes narrowed as he took a step toward him. "But you weren't." His voice rose as he turned and waved a hand around the room. "Your family didn't abandon you. You're the one who walked away from us. Numerous times."

Micah balled his hand into a fist and leveled Jake with a glare, fighting to keep the growl out of his voice. "And why do you think that was, Jake?"

Pushing to his feet, Dad cleared his throat and moved between them. "Boys."

The single word spoken sternly, yet quietly, was enough for Jake to take a step back. He dropped onto the couch next to his wife and cradled his head in his hands.

Micah dragged his hand over his face. "I've been living in Pittsburgh since I left Walter Reed. I stayed with a buddy for a while, but then he moved back to South Carolina to be with his family. Through Ian, I became involved in Phil's program."

"What sort of program requires you to sleep on park benches?"

"Jake!" Tori elbowed her husband.

Micah's eyes roamed over his family, taking in his young niece watching her uncles with wide eyes and his nephews ignoring the adults' conversation, and tempered the urge to light into his brother. Especially in front of their family. He wasn't a brawler anymore, no matter how much Jake's self-righteous attitude got under his skin. "Jake, your problem is you see only what you want. Not everything is black-and-white."

"I saw a picture of my brother sleeping on a park bench."

"Just because I was on that park bench doesn't mean I was sleeping. Or homeless, for that matter. I hung out with that homeless community for a while, sure. Not because I didn't have a place to live. But because it was the best way to connect with them. A lot of those guys have sacrificed so much for their country. They came home battered and beaten by what they fought so hard to protect, only to continue to spiral downward once they left the routine and discipline of the military.

"Despite programs in place to help veterans, some have fallen through the cracks. And not all of them had people in their corner, family to help support them through their traumas. Some of those guys needed a listening ear, to talk to someone who understands what they're going through. What it's like to come home with body parts missing. So while it may have appeared like I was sleeping on a park bench, there's more to the story. If I showed up in clean jeans, a tucked-in shirt and shiny new kicks, they wouldn't come near me. I went to them as they were. Sometimes I'd take food, an extra change of clothes, a cup of coffee, and I'd listen."

Shaking his head, Jake held up a hand. "I'm sorry, man. I served over there, too. I remember what it was like. I lost my best friend over there."

"While you may understand what that pit was like, at least you didn't leave any body parts back in the sand."

"How did Ian know to connect you with Phil?"

"I've stayed in touch with Ian since I left for basic training."

A muscle jumped in the side of Jake's jaw. "But not your own family? Don't you remember we developed the Fatigues to Farming program with you in mind?"

"And I never asked you to do that, Jake." Micah balled his fingers into a fist again. "Ian didn't accuse me of things beyond my control. Ian didn't judge me for past mistakes. Ian didn't refer to me as Micah the Menace. And when I needed help, I called Ian because I wanted more than a lecture." He unclenched his fingers and scrubbed his hand over his face. "You know what? Forget I said anything. Partnering with your program would be a mistake."

Micah turned and kissed Claudia on the cheek. "Thanks for dinner, C."

She grabbed his arm. "You're leaving?"

"I think that's for the best." He needed time to cool off before words flew out of his mouth that he couldn't take back.

"Stay. You're an important part of this family. Let us help you with whatever you need." Words spoken quietly, her eyes pleaded with him.

"Thanks. Maybe next time."

As he strode through the house and out the front door, the truth kicked Micah in the chest—there wouldn't be a next time. He didn't fit in with his family, and partnering with them wouldn't be an option.

He'd make the transitional home work because he'd made a promise. But he'd have to do it on his own—without his family's support.

Chapter Four

One month away from the clinic, and Paige was losing her touch.

Or perhaps it was the lack of sleep. Or the grief still weighing heavily on her.

Whatever her problem, she had to get over it, because her clients required her to be at her best. Somebody needed to claim a victory for today, even if it was a small win.

And that meant helping Dillon, her very wiggly client with developmental delays and a sensory processing disorder, with achieving his goal of dressing himself.

But the four-year-old had other plans about staying in his cozy John Deere–green pajamas printed with tractors.

"Dillon, show me how well you can get dressed today. Then we can add stickers to your chart."

Once Paige started working with Dillon in his

home, she guided Salina, his mother, in creating small milestones to encourage developing his skills toward achieving her son's ADL—activities of daily living. Which meant Salina had to stop doing what Dillon needed to learn for himself.

And today's session began with guiding him toward the goal of dressing himself independently. If they had time left in their one-hour therapy session, she hoped to do some fine motor activities with him, but a glance at her watch showed that might need to happen later in the week.

"Can't. Too tired." He lay on the carpeted floor, pushing a small tractor around his farm play set, complete with a red-and-white barn and matching silo.

"Oh, that's too bad. I have a surprise to show you, but if you're too tired to get dressed, maybe I should go so you can take a nap." She stood and moved away from his toddler bed made up with a comforter printed with farm animals.

The little boy with straight white-blond hair and large green eyes scrambled off the floor and stood in front of her. With his small fists on his hips, he glared at her and puffed out his bottom lip. "No nap."

She stretched out her hand. "Okay, no nap. How about if I help you take your arms out of your pajama shirt? Then you can show me how well you can pull it off your head?"

His shoulders slumped as he kicked a bare toe against the carpet.

At this rate, they were going to be there until lunchtime. But she needed to remain positive and patient.

She touched the hem of his shirt. "When you get dressed, then I will show you my surprise."

"What surprise?"

She pulled her phone out of the front pocket of her maroon scrub pants. "I took pictures of some goats this morning, and I'd like to show them to you once you get dressed."

Dillon lunged for her phone, but she held it back. "Clothes, then goats."

Still smiling, she waved a hand over his navy sweatpants, red sweatshirt and navy ankle socks with red heels that Salina had laid out on his bed. "Let's work together. Each time you help, I'll show you one picture of a goat. Then once you're all dressed, you can see the video I took of them. How does that sound?"

He gave her a long look, then swiped the clothes off the bed and plopped on the floor beside her. "Socks first."

With the heel pointing up, he tried to jam his toes into the opening, but they got caught on the edge of the material. Scrunching up his face, he pulled harder, but the sock wouldn't budge. He let out a wail and flung himself back, his head crashing into his fenced-in plastic farm animals. "Can't do it."

Careful to protect herself from his flailing arms, Paige knelt beside him, slid her hand under his back and guided him to a sitting position. "Yes, you can. We'll do it together. Look at your sock and touch the heel part."

Sniffing, he jabbed a finger at the red square.

"Great job. Show me the heel of your foot."

Rolling his head from side to side, Dillon lifted his foot and touched his heel.

"Way to go, buddy." She lifted her palm to him, and he slapped it.

A grin spread across his face.

Okay, tiny victory. But she'd take it.

Sitting next to him, Paige reached for the sock, turned it so the heel faced down, then gathered half of the fabric between her fingers. She looked at Dillon. "If your heel is on the bottom of your foot, then let's cover it up with the red part of your sock." She slid his toes into the sock the right way. "Put your fingers by mine and pull it over your foot so the red part is in the right spot."

Biting down on his tongue, he pulled his knee to his chest and followed her fingers. Once the sock covered his foot, he thrust his arms in the air. "I did it!"

"Hooray! Yes, you did! I knew you could." She high-fived both palms, then reached for his other sock. "Show me how well you can do it again."

With slow, deliberate movements, he moved his fingers along with her verbal cues and put his other sock on without any upsets. And they celebrated with another round of high fives.

After showing him pictures of Rosie and Daffy—one picture for each sock success—and wanting to take advantage of his excited attitude, Paige held his pajama top while he removed his arms and tugged it over his head. With each victory, she gave him another high five and then helped him slip his arms through the sleeves of his sweatshirt. Once he pulled the shirt down over his stomach, he jumped to his feet and grinned.

Paige wanted to do a happy dance. It had taken more than a week to get this far.

They swapped out his pajama pants for his sweatpants, and when he pulled them up, he gave her the sweetest smile that melted her heart. "I did it, Miss Paige."

"Yes, you sure did, buddy. I'm so proud of what you accomplished." Pushing to her feet, she held out a hand. "Let's show your mom what a great job you did."

"Can I watch the video now?"

"Yes, in the kitchen."

Hand in hand, they walked down the narrow hall strewn with books and toys and headed into the small kitchen that smelled of chocolate chip cookies.

Salina looked up from scooping cookie dough on trays. Her eyes widened, and her mouth curved into an O.

"Look, Mommy." Dillon patted his chest with both hands. "I did it."

Smiling brightly, she clapped, then hurried over to him and cupped both of his cheeks in her hands. "You did such a great job. I knew you could do it."

Pulling him to her chest, Salina looked over the top of his head at Paige, her dark brown eyes shimmering. She mouthed, "Thank you."

Paige nodded and returned the smile.

And this was why she loved her job so much. And why she needed to get her center going—to provide hope for her families as they worked together to achieve their goals. With more space, she could offer more opportunities to other families in the community.

"I told Dillon when he dressed himself, he could watch a goat video on my phone." Paige pulled out her phone once again and found the video she'd made that morning while doing chores. She knelt on the floor beside Dillon to show him the video. "I now own a goat farm."

While Dillon held the phone and giggled over Lulu, Rosie and Daffy playing tag in the barn, Paige pushed to her feet and faced Salina. "I'm creating an animal-assisted therapy practice for children like Dillon who don't respond well to a typical clinic environment."

"And you're using goats? Is that safe? Or even clean?"

"I know it doesn't sound like typical therapy practices, but yes, it is safe with the right goats who have been trained to interact with people, especially small children. They will be healthy and clean in the therapy barn."

"Barn?" Salina wrinkled her nose.

"A barnlike environment. I believe the children who need therapy services may respond well in a more natural environment. The therapy barn will have a kitchen for cooking, a playroom for private therapy sessions, a gym and an outdoor area with gardens to give them more opportunities to develop their skills."

"Sounds like you planned it out well."

"Yes, and under the guidance of Dr. O'Brien, who is advising me on the project."

"Well, I don't have to see it to know it's going

to be great. When Dillon had that meltdown at the hospital after Dr. O'Brien closed his practice and you offered to work with him at home, I knew you were an answer to prayer. I'm sure other families will feel the same way, too."

Paige's cheeks warmed. She squeezed Salina's hand. "Thank you for saying so. Children will learn and thrive where they feel safe, loved and comfortable. My program will offer that. With Dillon's love of farm animals, it may be a great fit for him."

And after today's win, Paige was more encouraged than before to stay focused on what needed to be done. She couldn't allow other distractions—namely Micah—to deter her from her goals.

Micah needed one person to pick up the phone and say yes.

Available contractors during the summer months were about as scarce as hen's teeth, as Ian used to say, but now that it was winter and many did interior work, Micah was still trying to find someone to meet with him. When Micah sat down after breakfast with one of Ian's old phone books, he hadn't expected the job to take all morning. But everyone he'd called so far was unavailable.

How was he going to keep his promise to

Paige about pulling his own weight if he was struggling to get started?

If he could do the work himself, he wouldn't need to ask for help, but that wasn't possible.

Asking his family was out of the question after the Sunday dinner blowup.

So now he needed to figure out a solution, because his next deadline with Ginny was going to be here before he was ready for it. He couldn't let the pressure get to him.

Not to mention Paige's constant presence.

They'd spent several hours the night before going over each of their programs, making lists of what needed to be done. Then Paige helped Micah sketch out a very rough idea of the renovations that needed to be done. And they managed to do it without arguing.

Maybe there was hope for them yet.

But he didn't have time to think about her right now.

He had two more numbers to call, and if neither of those panned out, then he didn't know what he was going to do.

He punched in the next number, and the phone rang until it connected to voice mail.

Terrific.

He tapped the next number on his phone and waited as the phone rang in his ear. He was just about to end the call when a gruff voice sounded in his ear. "Lefty Construction. We do it right the first time."

"Yeah, hi. I'm looking to have some construction work done." Micah explained the situation to the guy on the other end of the phone. To his surprise, the man agreed to come out to the house to check things out.

Twenty minutes later, a pickup with a diesel engine rumbled into the driveway.

Micah stood on the front porch, his shoulder against the railing beam.

A man in a tan utility jacket, torn jeans and a stained sweatshirt jumped out of the driver's side. A lit cigarette hung out of his mouth. He flicked it in the driveway and crushed it beneath the toe of his worn work boot.

If Ian were alive, he'd demand the dude clean up his litter, but Micah was desperate for a contractor, and he couldn't risk the guy driving off before they had a chance to talk.

The man strode to the porch, the stench of cigarette smoke arriving ahead of him. He extended his right hand, and Micah looked at it a minute before turning his arm and awkwardly shaking it. "George Pickens, but everyone calls me Lefty."

"Micah Holland. Thanks for coming so quickly."

They headed into the house, and Micah took

him into the kitchen, where the roughed-out plans were spread across the table. Micah explained what needed to be done.

Lefty pulled a pair of dingy reading glasses from his chest pocket and perched them on the bridge of his nose. He perused the plans, making noises to himself.

Micah half expected the guy to take some sort of notes, but he simply nodded, unclipped the tape measure from his belt and started measuring doorways and counter height, and then he walked from room to room muttering to himself. He pulled out a stubby carpenter pencil and made notes on Micah's drawings.

After they toured the upstairs and headed out to the front porch, Lefty removed his grungy baseball hat and scratched his head. "I'll run some numbers and get back to you. Just so you know, the work you want done ain't gonna be cheap."

"Yes, I know. You're insured, correct? And you'll handle acquiring all the permits?"

Lefty narrowed his eyes. "What kind of business do you think I'm running? Of course I'm insured. And my crew will take care of the necessary permits."

"Are you familiar with ADA regulations, because any work that needs to be done must be compliant."

"Yup. We'll take care of all that, too. My ma's been in a wheelchair since I was ten, so I'm aware."

Once they concluded their meeting, Lefty headed to his truck, then backed out of the driveway and barreled down the road.

As his taillights disappeared over the hill, Micah released a long-winded sigh.

Finally. He was headed in the right direction.

As Micah headed for the front door, bleating came from the backyard. Instead of going into the house, he rounded the side and shook his head. "Not again."

The goats had found another escape route and browsed on the dead vegetation sticking up from the snow around the lip of the pond. He pulled out his phone, and his thumb hovered over his father's name in his recent calls.

Micah really didn't want to ask his family for help, especially after the way he'd left them the other day, but what choice did he have?

Paige was working, and repairing the fence wasn't something Micah could do easily on his own.

He tapped on Dad's name.

"Holland Family Farm, Chuck speaking."

"Hey, Dad, anyone around to lend a hand? Paige's goats got out again. I can get them back to the barn, but the fence needs to be secured, and I can't do it by myself."

Man, he hated admitting that.

"Not a problem, Micah. Jake just walked in. I'll give Evan a call. Tuck's on duty at the fire station, but between the four of us, we can make sure they can't escape."

Closing his eyes, Micah clenched the phone. He hated the helpless feeling that swept over him. "Thanks, I appreciate it."

Less than ten minutes later, the farm truck drove past the house and backed into the barnyard.

With one of the pygmy goats under his arm, Micah strode across the grass to meet his dad and brothers.

Dad took the animal from him and carried it into the barn. Jake walked the perimeter of the fence, pulling on a pair of leather gloves while Evan fist bumped Micah. "Hey, man. What's going on?"

"It's been a day. After making a dozen calls, I finally met with a contractor who's willing to work up a quote. After our meeting, I found four goats out by the pond. Paige and I fixed a hole in the fence the other day, but the goats must've found another weak spot. The whole thing needs to be replaced. That's one of our first goals."

Evan eyed him. "Our?"

"Forced partnership, thanks to Ian."

Jake tracked back to them and nodded to Micah. "Little brother."

Jake never called Tucker or Evan "little brother." But his constant use of it with Micah reminded him of his place in the family—the runt still running to catch up.

"Jake."

Evan's eyes bounced between them.

"I found the hole. It won't take much to fix it, then we can walk the fence line and see if there are other areas that need to be reinforced. That'll buy you some time until the whole thing can be replaced."

"Thanks, man. I appreciate it."

"You met with a contractor? Who?"

"George Pickens of Lefty Construction."

"Be careful." A muscle jumped in Jake's jaw. "That dude's been known to cut corners."

"Not sure I have many other options. He answered his phone. I'm going to round up the other goats, and then I'll catch up to you."

Dad came out of the barn. "I'll give you a hand."

Jake and Evan headed to the truck and unloaded fencing supplies, shouldering rolls of wire, while Micah and his father headed toward the pond.

Dad chuckled. "When Betsy was alive, she

always threatened to have stew for dinner every time the goats browsed near the gardens around the pond."

"Mom was the same way. Remember the time one of the goats escaped and decided to feast on her lilac bush that bordered the yard near the barn? She was spitting mad when she called up Ian to get his goat."

It felt good to laugh at a memory of his mom instead of letting grief and guilt overwhelm him.

They reached the edge of the pond. Dad scooped up two goats, one in each arm, and tucked them gently against his chest, as if he were holding his grandchildren. The last goat, seeing it might be losing its final precious moments of freedom, made a run for it, scampering over the bridge Ian had constructed over the narrow end of the pond.

Micah strode after it, careful not to slip on the thin layer of ice, not really in the mood to play a game of tag with the animal. "Get back here, you little menace."

The goat stopped, looked at Micah, then bleated as if to challenge him. "Meh."

How did Ian used to call his goats?

Micah racked his brain, but he couldn't remember. "Here, Goaty Goaty. Want a treat?"

"Daffy, come."

Micah whipped around to find Paige standing behind him wearing a parka with a faux fur–lined hood, maroon scrubs and a pair of winter boots with side buttons. Her auburn hair had been piled on top of her head in some sort of messy knot. She slid up her sunglasses and rattled the can she held.

The goat raced past Micah and stopped in front of Paige. A wide grin spread across her face.

Micah shook his head. "Don't even…"

"What?" Paige picked up Daffy, then clamped a hand over her own mouth. But she wasn't fast enough for the bubble of laughter that managed to escape.

Another time, and Micah may have found humor in the situation, but his frustration with the events of the day soured his mood. He really needed to snap out of it. He couldn't let every little thing get to him.

"The goats escaped again. Dad, Jake and Evan came down to fix another hole."

The grin slid off Paige's face. "I'm sorry, Micah. I'll pay for any damage the goats have done."

Shaking his head, he waved away her words. "Forget it. But we do need to replace the fence as soon as possible."

"We?" She eyed him with a small smile on her face.

"Yes, we. We're in this together, remember?"

"How could I forget?"

Micah fell in step next to Paige as they headed back to the barn. "Hey, if it's too much for you, we can both walk away and wash our hands of the whole lot."

Paige nudged his shoulder with her own. "Walking away is your MO, Micah. Not mine. I finish what I start. And I need this—my clients need it. I just spent a very rewarding hour encouraging a little boy with delays to dress himself. And for the first time in a week, he did it. It was so exciting. Something we tend to take for granted, yet it's been a struggle for him for so long. So, the sooner we work through our goals, the quicker I can have a better program in place for children like him." The glow in her eyes ignited something in his chest.

He understood that passion, that desire to do more for those they cared about.

"In a hurry to get rid of me?"

"No. I'm just tired." She waved a hand over the pens. "This feels very overwhelming. Ian handled the day-to-day stuff. I just came to play with the goats. But now I'm up at four every morning to feed and water them. I need to clean the barn, schedule in hoof trimming and de-worming, order feed. Let's just say, I'm feeling very unqualified."

"I hear you. I feel like a toddler clomping around in his father's shoes. Or in this case, Ian's shoes. There's no way I can measure up."

She buried her face in Daffy's neck. "Maybe we're not supposed to fill someone else's shoes. Maybe we're supposed to make our own steps."

"It'd be nice to have a clue."

"True dat."

Micah grinned at the unexpected slang coming from Ms. Type A. "Ian wasn't a fool, and he was of sound mind. He knew what he was doing even if we don't. Thankfully, everything doesn't have to happen overnight. And we're not doing it alone. I know you think I don't follow through, but you can count on me, Paige."

She looked at him with an unreadable expression. Then she rested a hand on one of the fence posts. "I know how important this is to you, Micah. You have a lot at stake as well. I'll help however I can."

"Know any contractors looking for work? I think I called every number listed in Ian's old phone book. Nearly everyone's booked. Lefty Construction is going to run some numbers…"

"I sense a *but*."

"Jake mentioned the guy's been known to cut corners. While I can't risk inferior work, no one else was able to take my call, either."

"What about your family? They're great at

pitching in. And they'd know the regs after having the cabins built for the Fatigues to Farming program."

Micah's gaze drifted down the road, where four small cabins sat in a grove of pines. "No. They're busy with their families, work and everything else. I'm not going to be the pesky little brother who constantly needs help. I'll work this out."

Before they could say anything else, Jake and Evan returned with their tools and dumped everything in the bed of the truck. "The fence is secure for now, but you will need to replace it."

"Thanks, guys. How can I repay you?" Paige asked.

Jake and Evan looked at one another, then grinned. "You still make those coconut-pecan cookies dipped in chocolate?"

"Yes, want a batch?"

Jake and Evan looked at each other once more, then spoke in unison, each holding up two fingers. "A double batch."

Paige laughed and wrapped them together in a hug. "You got it. It's the least I can do. Let me know how much I owe for the fencing."

"The cookies will cover it."

Their easy banter showed how comfortable Paige was around his family. She'd known them her whole life, but this easygoing teasing spiked an edgy feeling in his gut.

Jealousy?

No, this was something different. A longing that crept over Micah.

She belonged, and he didn't. But he had no one to blame but himself.

He meant what he'd said to Paige—he planned to stick around for the long haul. Maybe then he could change the deep-seated opinion others seemed to have about him.

Chapter Five

Paige was wasting her energy.

If Micah wasn't going to accept the help she was offering, then she could find a better use of her time. Especially with meeting her own deadlines.

No one exasperated her like he did.

"Micah, I'm trying to help, but you're being stubborn."

"Me? Stubborn? Paige, I didn't ask for you to come and take over. I'm perfectly capable of wrapping a few dishes."

"You called and asked if I knew of anyone who could give you a hand packing up Ian and Betsy's things before demolition begins."

"Right—meaning give me suggestions. Don't railroad me into doing it your way."

"I'm not taking over. I'm here to help." She needed to keep her cool and show she could be reasonable, too. Even if he didn't want to listen. Pulling on her years of training from working with defiant clients, Paige pushed away her annoyance and schooled her tone. "Like it or not, we're in this together, and in order to succeed, we need to work as a team. I have the afternoon free, so I can lend a hand with some of the packing."

Dressed in faded jeans, a gray flannel shirt, and slip-on leather shoes, he stood with his back to her, his left hand resting against the cluttered buffet in Ian's dining room. "I don't want you to think I'm incompetent."

She frowned. "What? I don't think that at all." She rubbed a hand across her forehead. "I'm sorry if I gave that impression. But, listen, Micah—we need to figure out a way to get along for the sake of getting both of our programs up and running. You don't have to like me, but at least try to hear what I'm saying."

He pivoted, a deep frown etched in his forehead. "What are you talking about? Of course I like you. Why would you think otherwise?"

She lifted a shoulder. "You argue with me over everything. And you're so competitive."

Micah laughed, a lush, deep sound that bounced off the faded flowered wallpaper. "That's rich. More like the pot calling the kettle black, don't you think?"

"Wanting to do my best doesn't mean I'm competitive."

"Whatever." He crossed the room and held out his hand. "Truce?"

She took it, his skin warm. "Truce. I have a friend who owns a cleaning and home organization business. After Betsy died, CJ cleaned weekly for Ian, so she's familiar with the house. How about if I call her and see if she can organize a crew to handle the packing? Even though you disagree with storing everything, we can do it until the house is finished, then pull it out and go through it. Otherwise, it's going to take us a lot more time to go through all of Ian and Betsy's belongings when we need to be moving forward with meeting our goals."

Micah heaved a sigh and gave her a look of resignation. "Okay, fine. Give her a call. I still say we should donate all of it instead of storing, but at least it will give me time to figure out what to do with all this junk. Why do people need so much stuff anyway?" He waved his hand toward the china closet. "Take that, for example. Betsy has a whole cabinet full of teacups. She could only use one at a time."

Paige bit back a grin. "She used to host teas every spring and Christmas. She'd invite my grandma, my mom, my sister and me. Your mom used to come, too. We wore our prettiest dresses, and she set the table with lacy table-cloths and fabric napkins, and we'd have tea, savories and sweets. I always felt so grown-up to be drinking tea with the other ladies."

Micah scratched the back of his head. "Sounds like a sweet memory."

"It was."

"Why don't you take them?" He opened the china closet door, reached for one of the dainty teacups and handed it to her. "Take the teacups, teapots…all of it."

She cradled the translucent cup in her hand. "And do what with it? My cottage is barely bigger than a shoebox. I don't have space for them."

"Carry on that legacy—have tea parties with your clients, with your family, whoever you want. I think it would make Betsy happy to know her teacups were being used again."

"Teacups and goat therapy. Not so sure that tea parties in a barn is a good combination."

"Why not?"

"It's not very practical."

"Sometimes you need to move past practicality. Think about how you felt at those tea parties. Imagine how much joy you could bring to some of your clients."

"I don't know, Micah. There are safety issues to consider. Those cup handles are going to be tough for some of my clients to even grasp. And what if one of them gets dropped and broken? Someone could get injured."

Micah shrugged. "It gets swept up and thrown away. Come on, Paige, think outside the box for once. We can always find adaptive cups for those who need them, but just imagine how tea parties will make your clients feel. I think Betsy would back me up, too."

"You just want to get rid of them."

He grinned. "Well, there's that, too."

Since he gave in to her storage idea, maybe she needed to give in, too.

She flung her hands in the air. "Okay, fine. Thank you. I'll grab some packing material from the kitchen and start wrapping them."

"No rush. I'm not going anywhere."

So he said. What would it take for her to take him at his word?

She returned with packing material and a couple of sturdy boxes. Opening the door to the china closet, she reached for a pale blue teacup with a curved handle and roses around the rim. She wrapped it carefully and handed it to Micah. By working together, they emptied the china closet in record time.

She headed to the kitchen and washed her hands. Eyeing the sink full of dirty dishes, she called to him, "Want me to give you a hand with these?"

He headed into the kitchen and leaned against the counter. "Nah, I bought a handled sponge and brush so I could take care of them. I'm having a dishwasher installed when the kitchen gets redone, which will make cleanup much easier."

"Good idea." She glanced at her smart watch. "I need to feed and water the goats."

"Want a hand?" Micah grinned. "That's all I have to offer."

"Sure. Doing the chores by myself takes much longer."

"Why not ask for help? Or hire someone? I'm sure there's a teenager around here who wouldn't mind making a few extra bucks."

"I can handle it."

"Again with the double standard. Since I have only one arm, I need help. But you have two arms, so you're perfectly capable of carrying the world on your shoulders all by yourself, right?"

"I never said that, and if you want to twist my words, then go ahead, but that's on you. I've had to learn to take care of myself. That's just how it was."

Micah reached for her arm. "Hey, you're not alone anymore. We're in this together, remember?"

"So you keep saying. Problem is, Micah, I'm still struggling to trust you to stick around."

"You have no clue who I am anymore. You're

still stuck with the image of the old Micah. People change, Paige. You just have to be willing to look beyond the past to see it." He lifted his coat off the back of the chair, shrugged into it and headed outside, the door slamming behind him.

Grabbing her own coat, she hurried after him. As she closed the door behind her, a red SUV pulled in the driveway behind Micah's black one.

Jake's wife, Tori, stepped out of the driver's side, then opened the back door and removed a baby carrier. Spying them, she lifted a gloved hand and waved as she headed toward the porch. "Hey, guys."

"Hey, Tori. What's going on?" Micah dropped a kiss on his sister-in-law's cheek.

"Well, I had an idea I wanted to run by the two of you if you have a minute?"

Micah opened the door. "Sure, let's get Charlie in out of the cold."

Inside the house, Micah directed them to the living room. "Have a seat. Want a drink or something?"

"No, thanks. I know you're busy, so I won't take up much of your time." Tori removed her coat and gloves, then pulled the blanket off Charlie's carrier. She lifted the infant out of his seat, then glanced at Micah. "Want to hold him?"

Micah's eyes widened. "Me? I…" He glanced at his left arm. "I don't know…"

"Sure, you can." Tori sat on the couch, then patted the cushion beside her. Once Micah sat, she settled the baby in the curve of his arm. "Wrap your arm around his body and place your hand on his legs."

Paige slipped her phone out of her back pocket and took a picture of Charlie staring at his uncle with his large blue eyes.

Paige's heart turned to jelly as Micah brushed his lips across his nephew's forehead. "What do you think, little man? You like hanging out with your uncle Micah?"

Tori tugged on Charlie's pant legs, covering his exposed skin. "You look great with him. Someday, you'll have your own to cuddle."

A shadow passed over Micah's face. Then he leaned forward and nearly pushed Charlie back into his mother's arms. "What did you want to talk about?"

Cradling her son, Tori stood and looked at both of them. "I would like to organize a marketing and fund-raising campaign to raise awareness for your programs like I did for the Fatigues to Farming program."

Micah and Paige exchanged glances, then he jerked his attention to Tori. "Why?"

"I told you—to help market your programs

and to raise money. We had great success with the Fatigues to Farming campaign in securing long-term donors who wanted to partner with our program."

Micah scratched the back of his head. "I don't know, Tori. I appreciate you thinking of us and all, but I'm not sure that's the best direction to take."

"Why not?" Paige folded her arms over her chest and shot him a look.

"Because Ian left us a sizable trust to put toward our programs."

"Yes, and that was extremely generous, but that money will run out soon with all the remodeling. With your program being a nonprofit, an awareness campaign can help you secure donors willing to partner with you on a regular basis. Maybe God is using Tori to be a part of that process."

Tori rested a hand on his shoulder. "Micah, you are an inspiration. Tell your story to inspire others."

"I don't want anyone's pity or misplaced inspiration because of my disability." He turned to face them and waved a hand toward Paige. "Especially when there are people, like Paige, who work tirelessly to help children learn and strengthen their skills."

Her eyes shot up and searched his face as her cheeks warmed.

Tori adjusted Charlie on her shoulder. "You're both uniquely qualified to be the voices someone else needs to hear. Let me help amplify what you have to say."

Paige stepped forward and held out her hands toward the baby. "May I hold him?"

Nodding, Tori passed her son to Paige, who curled him against her chest. Her eyes roamed over his tiny features, and she swallowed a sigh.

Someday, maybe, she'd have children of her own. In the meantime, she'd get her fix through other people's.

Even though she wanted nothing more than to focus on the precious infant in her arms, she needed to find some way to convince Micah—once again—that Tori's suggestion was a good one. She leveled him with a direct look. "What are you afraid of?"

He waved away her words. "I'm not afraid of anything."

"Then why not do this? I understand you don't want misplaced inspiration, but what you fail to see is you *are* an inspiration. Not because you lost an arm, but because of the size of your heart. You want these men to have a better life, then let others help so you can offer even more resources. Tell your story and allow it to reflect

God's glory and the way He's worked in your life to bring you to this point. *That's* what makes you an inspiration."

Micah dragged his hand through his hair, then shot a look at Tori. "What does Jake have to say about this?"

"Jake?" Tori frowned. "I haven't talked to him, but I know he'd be all for it."

Micah raised an eyebrow. "You sure about that? You heard him the other day at the farmhouse."

A shadow passed over Tori's eyes, and she took a step back. "Oh, Micah. There's so much that you don't know. You and your brother really need to talk."

"I know what Jake thinks of me. No sense in reopening old wounds."

"That wound hasn't even closed for it to reopen. It's been festering for years, infecting your perception."

Paige handed Charlie back to his mother, then stood in front of Micah. "I have an idea. What if we didn't do a large event like the Fatigues to Farming fund-raiser? What about an open house instead? Once the house and the therapy barn are ready, we can have a party. Talk about our programs to family and friends and allow word of mouth to be our advertising."

Micah looked at her with something akin to

relief in his eyes. Then he nodded. "All right. I'd be willing to do something on a smaller scale. As long as your center was a part of it, too."

Finally.

She grinned and threw her arms around his neck. "You won't be sorry."

Micah's hand gripped her waist, and the look on his face caused her heart to trip against her ribs.

Where had that come from?

Taking a step away from him, she gripped the heart on her necklace and gave a little laugh that sounded tinny to her ears. "Well, Tori, it looks like you have an open house to plan. Let me know how I can help."

Especially if Micah truly meant it about sticking around. After spending a week with Micah—more time than she had in the past eight years combined—she realized she liked having him around. And she wasn't ready for another painful goodbye.

Seriously? How did two people acquire so much stuff?

Maybe it was his minimalist living since enlisting in the army—everything he owned could fit in a duffel—but it seemed like Ian and Betsy didn't get rid of much. Not exactly hoarders. More like clutterbugs, as his mom used to say.

Micah had to give Paige credit—her suggestion to hire her friend with the cleaning company was the right choice.

Cassidy Jenson's organizational skills deserved awards, and her team managed to clean out the first floor in record time.

While they boxed up everything on the second floor, Micah headed to the attic to see what he could do to start clearing that space. Not only did it need to be emptied for the electrician to do the rewiring, but Micah planned to live up there in order to leave the bedrooms for the men.

Right now, it felt like a meat locker. But insulation and drywall would take care of that.

Standing at the top with his back to the only window, he stared at the long room that went the whole length of the house. His eyes bounced off towers of boxes, discarded furniture and an assorted collection of odds and ends that filled every nook of the space.

He had no idea where to begin.

The grimy window offered little light. A chill slithered down Micah's spine. The confined air smelled musty, of trapped memories longing to be shared, used belongings gathering dust and possessions without owners.

Stacks of red and green totes in one corner were most likely Christmas decorations, and clear plastic containers held all different colors of yarn. Maybe Claudia would know of someone at church who could use it. Boxes marked "books" had been stacked on top of each other. Old furniture, used small appliances and bags of clothes had been piled in any available space.

Did Ian get rid of anything?

Two long white tables sat in the middle of the room, with rolls of brightly colored fabric stacked on shelves behind them. A white sewing machine sat on one end. A worn wooden office chair had been pulled away from the table, as if someone had left and expected to return.

Only that wasn't going to happen.

Ian wasn't coming back, and now it was up to Micah to find someone else to fill that seat.

He approached the table and picked up a piece of nylon material cut in a diamond shape. He moved to the other side of the table and picked up a box kite in various shades of blue.

His phone chimed in his front pocket. He pulled it out to find a text from Paige. You home? I have something for you.

Yes. Working in Ian's attic. Come on up.

See you in a few.

He shoved his phone in his back pocket and picked up another kite—this one done in reds, yellows and oranges. He went through the stack. There had to be at least thirty in various shapes and sizes piled between the other side of the table and the sloped wall.

What was Ian doing with all these kites? And why hadn't he mentioned them before?

Micah rounded the table, and his foot slid on something. He reached down and picked up a smudged, wrinkled, torn sheet of paper. Turning it over, he found an old advertisement that had lost its gloss for Shelby Lake's annual kite festival.

Man, he hadn't been to the festival since high school. After he entered the kite-flying event, he ended up going kite-to-kite with Paige, and she'd never let him forget her victory over him.

On the very bottom, in fine print, he read, "Thanks to Ian and Betsy Wilder for their creation and donation of the kites to the festival."

Well, that explained a lot.

"Micah?" Paige called from the bottom of the steps.

"Up here."

The stairs creaked as she walked up. She stood at the top, still wearing her parka, unzipped and hanging open. Dressed in jeans and a blue-and-white-striped pullover sweater, and with her auburn hair pulled back into a ponytail, she looked eighteen all over again. Hands on hips, she surveyed the large room. "I'd forgotten how big this attic was."

"Yeah, the mice and spiders seem to be enjoying it. Somehow, I need to turn this into a living space. As soon as I learn to duck. I've lost count how many times I've hit my head on this lower peak. Not to mention the sauna-type heat in the summer and polar vortex temps in the winter."

"Good insulation will take care of that." Rubbing her hands over her arms, Paige crossed the room to the table and ran a finger over the yellowed machine. "This is Betsy's serger. I haven't seen this in years. I figured Ian had gotten rid of it."

"Serger?"

"It's a type of sewing machine that trims and encloses the seam as it sews. Seems as if Ian had been using it after she passed away."

"If you want it, you're welcome to take it. Did you know they made kites?"

Nodding, Paige reached for the orange-handled scissors. "After Betsy's arthritis affected her finger joints, my grandma and I used to come over and cut out kite material on her dining room table. Betsy told us how she and Ian met at a kite festival, and she hoped someday one of her kites would be used to bring another couple together."

Out of respect for the woman he'd loved like another grandmother, Micah resisted the urge to roll his eyes. "She was a romantic."

"I wonder when Ian moved everything up here." Paige returned the scissors to the table. "What are you going to do with this stuff?"

Still holding the outdated flyer, Micah glanced at it, then scanned the rolls of brightly colored fabric. He lifted a shoulder. "Maybe I should keep it. At least for a little while. Maybe one of the guys would like to get into kite making to carry on Ian's legacy."

"Wow, Micah Holland actually wants to keep something."

He rolled his eyes. "Maybe it's a stupid idea."

She pressed a hand against his arm. "Lighten up. I was teasing. Once the construction is finished, I can help you move everything to one of the first-floor rooms and outfit it with adaptive equipment."

He eyed her. "What sort of adaptive equipment?"

"Whatever is needed. Cushioned-grip scissors, magnifiers, low-level cutting tables and other tools to help, depending on what the need is."

"Thanks, Paige. Now I just need to figure out the best place."

"What about the sunporch? It's enclosed, insulated and offers a lot of natural light."

"Maybe. But in the meantime, I still need to get it out of here so the electrician can replace the knob and tube wiring before the attic is insulated. Otherwise, it will slow the process of other projects that need to be done."

"Once CJ's crew is finished with the second floor, we'll bring them up here and get this packed up, too." She reached into her tote bag, pulled out a slightly smushed paper bag, and handed it to him. "Here."

He took it. "What's this?"

"I made cookies for your brothers and dad, so I wrapped up some for you, too…as a thank-you, once again, for helping with the fence."

"That's kind of you, but not necessary." He opened the bag and released the scents of coconut, baked sugar and butter. Setting it on the table, he reached in, pulled out a cookie and took a bite. "I won't give back the cookies, though. These are great."

"Thanks. The chocolate-dipped coconut pecan is my grandma's recipe."

He finished the cookie in two bites, then brushed the crumbs off his fingers on the leg of his jeans. "I have something for you, too. When I was up here earlier trying to come up with some sort of a plan, I found a box of pictures and figured you'd like to go through them and take any you'd like to keep."

"Pictures of what?"

"Ian and Betsy. Some with you and your sister. Some with your grandparents. I pulled out the ones with my family." Swiping the cookie bag, he nodded toward the stairs, then followed her down.

"Speaking of family, things getting any better with yours? You and Jake seemed a bit stiff around each other yesterday."

"He's going to be my biggest hurdle. I don't know if things will ever be right with us. After Mom was killed, I enlisted to prove I wasn't as reckless and irresponsible as he claimed, only to show he was right after all." At the bottom of the stairs, Micah closed the door behind them, then walked into the kitchen.

"What do you mean?"

He opened the fridge and reached for the milk. Then he turned over two glasses on the drying mat and filled them. After putting the milk away, he handed a glass to Paige, then grabbed another cookie out of the bag and dunked it in his milk. He set his half-finished glass of milk on the kitchen table, then headed for the dining room. He returned with a small wooden box and handed it to her.

Instead of opening it, she looked at Micah, who snatched another cookie. "Let's go back to the previous conversation—what do you mean about Jake being right after all?"

He shook his head, not wanting to go there.

"Forget it. Jake and I put on a good show in front of Dad and my brothers, but he pities me. And that's the last thing I want from anyone."

"Maybe that's your perception."

Micah drained his glass. "Can we talk about something else, please? Such as where I'm going to put all the stuff in the attic? The house is becoming a construction zone, and there's no place for storage."

"Like I said—CJ's team can handle that, too." Paige laid a hand on his arm. "Just like you keep telling me—you're not in this alone."

His eyes drifted toward her long, narrow fingers with the trimmed, unpolished nails. Then he met her gaze. Paige was the one person he could count on to tell him like it was, the one person who refused to pity him. And now something shifted in his chest. He couldn't quite name it, but having someone like her in his corner gave him hope that maybe the next few months wouldn't seem as overwhelming with her by his side.

He just needed to make sure he didn't do anything to mess it up.

Chapter Six

Paige was in over her head.

In all the years she'd hung around Ian's farm, she'd never been around when the goats had been born—she simply cuddled them days after their birth.

Now, at four thirty in the morning, she had to figure out what to do, because this mama goat was clearly in distress and Paige's phone call to Willow, her best friend who was a veterinarian, had gone to voice mail.

The goat's pained bleating tore at Paige's heart.

The black-and-white Nigerian dwarf goat lay on her side on a bed of hay, her swollen abdomen pulsing.

Maybe she should call Micah.

With growing up on a farm, surely he'd know

what to do. She hated waking him up, though. But what else could she do?

And he *had* said he would help in any way he could.

Resting a hand on the goat's hip, Paige pulled her phone out of the back pocket of her jeans, set it on the floor and instructed the voice assistant to call Micah.

The phone rang on speakerphone, the sound bouncing off the walls in the wood barn.

"'Lo?" Micah's voice sounded gruff and gravelly.

"Micah, it's Paige. I'm in the barn…and I need your help." She curled her fingers around the silver heart lying against her throat.

"Paige? What are you doing in there?"

"Buttons is in labor, but there's a problem."

"Did you call the vet?"

"I called Willow, but it went straight to voice mail."

"We need to call Dr. Mary."

"I don't want to wake her if it's nothing."

Micah sighed through the phone. "I'll be right out."

The call ended.

A mix of relief and guilt washed over her.

A few minutes later, the barn door opened, and Micah strode in wearing jeans, an olive-green army sweatshirt and a baseball hat smashed against his dark curls. Lines edged his tired eyes, and his set jaw suggested he wasn't pleased by her phone call.

"I'm sorry for waking you up. I didn't know what else to do."

He waved away her words, then sat on the barn floor next to the goat. Wincing, he stretched out his right leg and rubbed his thigh. "Don't worry about it. Ian kept an emergency kit in the barn. Can you find it?"

Paige scurried to her feet and searched. She returned with the red bag. "I found it."

"Good, unzip it, please, and find me a glove. I want to check to be sure, but one of the kids may be breech. If so, Buttons may need some assistance delivering her babies."

"Babies? As in plural?"

"Yes, it's not uncommon for goats to have two kids. I figured you'd know that."

Even though his tone was neutral, his words made her realize, once again, how little she knew about caring for goats. She needed a crash course in Goating 101. Maybe then she wouldn't feel so overwhelmed.

Again, for the hundredth time—what had Ian been thinking?

Paige helped pull the arm-length glove onto his hand. Then, speaking softly, Micah ran his hand over the goat's side, careful not to spook her. After inspecting her, Micah sat back and Paige helped to remove the glove. "I can feel the kid's nose and two front feet, so the first one is delivering in the proper position. It may be taking some time, especially if Buttons is a first-time mom."

"I'm sorry for waking you up. She just looked so pained on the webcam."

"Webcam?"

Paige's cheeks warmed. "Since I don't live next to the barn, I set up a webcam so I could check on them. I'm sure that sounds silly to you."

"Actually, it's kind of smart. Most animals in labor don't need human intervention, but the delivery does take time. We need to let nature take its course."

"You should go back to bed. I can handle this." She waved a hand toward the barn door.

Or she'd do a quick online search and figure it out. Maybe that's what she should've done before waking him.

"Right." He shot her a look that showed he doubted her abilities. "I can't go back to sleep anyway."

"Why not?"

He dragged a hand over his face. "Your call pulled me out of a nightmare."

"I'm sorry. Want to talk about it?"

"Not really."

"It may help."

"I doubt it. I was reliving the night I lost my arm. There's nothing that can change that."

"Oh."

"Yeah."

"What happened?"

"In my nightmare? Or that night?"

She shrugged. "Whichever one you want to talk about."

"How about neither?"

"Okay. I won't pry anymore."

He sighed. "My team was out on routine patrol. A few miles from base, a boy about twelve or thirteen waved us down. There'd been an accident, and his older brother was hurt. He was crying and begged us to help him."

"Poor kid."

He gave her a hard look, his eyes stony. "Not by a long shot. We called it in, but the kid was nearly hysterical. All I could think was, what if one of my brothers was injured? Would I wait around or see what I could do to help?"

"What did you do?"

"I made a reckless choice." Micah stared ahead, his voice hollow. "I should've waited for more intel—I knew better, but I didn't listen to my instincts. When I rounded the bend where the supposed accident was, I realized we'd been set up. The so-called injured brother and a buddy opened fire and threw a homemade bomb at us. The last thing I remember was throwing myself on top of Corporal Wallace, one of the guys in our unit who tried to talk me into waiting. I woke up in a hospital in Germany five days later. Burns puckered my neck. My right arm was gone, and my right leg was a mess. The pain was so intense I begged God to let me die."

"Oh, Micah." She blinked back another surge of tears. He continued to stare as if lost in his memory, and the barn was suddenly so quiet, it felt as if they were the only two people for miles. She felt his vulnerability and his loss acutely, and a wave of empathy swamped her. "I can't even imagine what you've gone through. What about your friend? Did he survive?"

"He had a concussion and a few cracked ribs. The rest of the guys had minor injuries."

"You saved their lives. That's very heroic."

His head jerked up, his eyes flaming and jaw set. "Heroic? No way. I was reckless. What I did was irresponsible. Thanks to my carelessness, I destroyed my life. I got what I deserved."

The anguish on his face wrecked her.

She shook her head and reached for him. "No. You followed your heart. Those men are to blame—not you!"

"Whatever." He rubbed his right shoulder. "Nothing I can do about it now."

Buttons let out a crying bleat.

Micah dragged a hand over his face. "It's baby time. We'll let nature take its course and help only if necessary."

Paige sat next to Buttons and rubbed her side, her mind more focused on Micah's story than the goat. About ten minutes later, Buttons let out a louder bleat, and her abdomen rippled.

"Paige, grab one of those towels and be prepared to catch the kid. We need to get it dried off so it doesn't freeze."

She did as he instructed. A few minutes later, she caught the glistening kid in the clean towel and rubbed it dry.

"Lay it on the hay next to its mother."

Paige did so, and helped Micah deliver the second one as Buttons began cleaning the first kid.

Once the second one had been delivered, Paige set it gently next to its twin.

Her vision blurred as she watched the gentle way the mother cared for her babies. Sniffing, she ran a hand across her eyes and turned to Micah. "Thank you for being here. There's so much I need to learn about raising goats."

He looked at her with a softness in his eyes she hadn't seen in years. Then he leaned forward and brushed a tear off her cheek with the pad of his thumb. "It takes time, Paige. It won't happen overnight. Even for an overachiever like you."

Paige smiled and lowered her eyes. "Thank you for taking my call and being here to help me through this. I'm sure I overreacted."

"It happens. Listen, Ian has bookshelves packed with books on caring for goats. If Cassidy's crew hasn't packed them yet, you're welcome to them."

"That would be great, thanks. For everything." She reached over and gave his hand a tight squeeze.

He squeezed back, but instead of releasing her fingers, he rubbed his thumb over her skin. Micah's eyes darkened as he scanned her face. He shifted slightly, moving closer, and he leaned in—

Paige's cell phone rang in her pocket, startling her. Micah jerked back. She fumbled for it, her fingers trembling slightly. She answered, her voice slightly breathy. "Hello?"

"Paige, so sorry I missed your call. Somehow, the volume on my phone had gotten turned off. Is everything okay?" Willow's voice sounded through the phone.

"Yes, I overreacted about one of my goats giving birth."

"Giving birth? It's a little early in the season for that."

"This is one of the new Nigerian dwarf goats Ian purchased recently, and it was a surprise pregnancy."

"Do you want me to come and check things out?"

"We've got it under control, so no need to rush over here. If you're not busy later, you can swing by if you want."

"We? You're not alone?"

"No, Micah's here. He gave me a hand."

Willow chuckled softly. "I'm definitely staying put now."

Paige rolled her eyes. "'Bye, Will." She stowed her phone in her back pocket, then pushed to her feet.

Micah had stood and moved to the barn door.

She cast another glance at the doe caring for her kids. "I think we're done here. Hopefully you can go back to sleep."

Turning, he lifted a shoulder. "Nah, I'm up for the day. I have a bunch of stuff to do anyway. I'll just get an earlier start."

"I appreciate everything you did for me."

A slow smile spread across his face. "See, we can work together without bickering. There's hope for this partnership yet." He brushed a knuckle across her chin, then strode out of the barn whistling.

Watching him disappear into the house, Paige realized two things—her perception of Micah was way off, and her heart was definitely in trouble.

How could she get him to see beyond the pain of his past choices to show what a value he was to others? And to do it without getting her heart broken in the process?

All Paige wanted was to get the books Micah had offered and leave.

Even though CJ's crew had packed up everything, Micah had hauled the boxes of Ian's books out of storage for her.

She appreciated his thoughtfulness.

Then, after Salina had called to say Dillon was sick and she needed to cancel their therapy session for the day, Paige had decided to spend the rest of her unexpected free afternoon learning more about caring for the goats.

She intended to grab the books and leave, but Micah's phone had rung right after he opened the door.

Even though he had motioned her into the living room, then moved into the kitchen for privacy, she could still hear his end of the conversation. And it didn't sound good. Did he realize how much his voice carried when he was upset?

She didn't want to be listening in on his conversation. Other than coming back later, what other choice did she have?

So, while she pretended to be engaged in the books, his frustrated voice slammed into her chest. Especially after she'd learned about the tragedy that took his arm.

"Listen, Jerome, I know it's hard, man. I've been there. But you can do this. Phil believes in you. I believe in you. Stick with the program." He paused a moment. "Dude, listen to me. No, really listen, you're not ready to go back home. It's not healthy for you. Phil and his team will help you to grow stronger physically and mentally so you can go back to your family. Keep holding on. Love you, too, man. I'll talk to you tomorrow."

Paige pulled a book out of the box, then hurried to Betsy's chair near the window and pretended to read. Her eyes rested on a colorful picture of two goats, but her mind wrapped around Micah's words and the compassionate tone he'd used on the phone.

He really cared about those men. Judging from his responses, the person on the other end seemed to care about him as well.

Why was it so hard to reconcile the Micah

from her childhood with the man he'd become today?

Because she was afraid.

Childhood Micah annoyed her. Grown-up Micah…well, he intrigued her. And that was dangerous. At least for her.

She needed to keep him in a tidy little box so he couldn't inflict any damage. Because after the way he'd helped her with the kidding goat, she realized falling for him could happen so easily.

And neither of them needed that.

"Good read?"

His voice startled her. Heat suffused her face. She slammed the book shut, then jumped to her feet and turned to find him in the doorway, resting a shoulder against the doorjamb.

"I was just reading about—" she turned the book over and groaned "—101 Ways to Cook a Goat."

He raised an eyebrow and grinned. Pushing away from the doorway, he shoved his hand in his front pocket and crossed the room. "Was last night too much? Now you want to grill the goats?"

"No, not at all." She returned the book to the box, shoving it back into place. Then she turned back to Micah and crossed her arms over her chest. "I grabbed the book as I went by but I didn't pay attention to what I was reading. Why would Ian have a book like that anyway?"

He shrugged. "Probably for the same reason my dad has many cookbooks on how to cook beef. Despite how cute they may be, some farmers raise goats for meat."

"Not my goats."

"Maybe not the ones you use in your therapy program, but some breeds are designed to be eaten. And Ian used to have some for that purpose."

The idea made her stomach clench. "I just came today to pick up the books you mentioned."

"Yeah, I know. Sorry about the interruption. The phone call was unexpected."

"Everything okay?"

Micah dragged a hand over his face. "Yeah, I guess. Or at least it will be. One of the new guys I had started mentoring at the Next Step is having some issues acclimating to the program."

Paige folded the book against her chest and glanced at Micah. "Mind if I ask you a personal question?"

He lifted a shoulder. "Go for it."

"Were you homeless? Is that why you want to turn this house into a transitional home?"

Micah sat on the edge of Ian's chair, his back to Paige and his head bent. "For a brief time.

After being discharged from the hospital, I planned to come back to Shelby Lake, but instead I made a last-minute decision to head to Pittsburgh to stay with a buddy from my squad, who offered to help me find a job. But honestly, my head was still a bit messed up. Rusty was a good dude. He let me crash at his place and suggested different ways to better myself—night school to further my education, counseling to help curb my anger. But I wasn't ready to hear it. I blew off the job, and after losing the second one, Rusty said if I wasn't going to work, I couldn't stay with him. So, instead of trying again, I left."

"Where did you go?" Her heart sank as she thought of him alone, confused, scared. He'd been through so much, and she'd been so cavalier in her judgments.

"I walked the streets for a couple of weeks and slept in shelters at night. They gave me a hot meal and a bed." Micah cupped a hand over his face. "I gotta say, it was the scariest time of my life. The gnaw of hunger never felt so real."

"Why didn't you come home? Your family would've moved mountains to help you. I know they spent months looking for you."

"Because I was ashamed. I was a dude without an address, but my pride kept me from reaching out to the one person who'd take me back in a heartbeat…my dad. When the man who ran the shelter broke his leg, I offered to help him out in exchange for room and board. When I wasn't helping at the shelter, I'd head to the streets and talk with some of the guys. Veterans like me, who had seen the worst and had the scars to prove it. I'd hand out clothes and blankets that had been donated. And just listen to them."

"You've always had a big heart." She said it softly, almost afraid to bestow such a compliment on him.

"A big heart doesn't get you very far."

"How so?"

"I met this guy who had hardly anything. The nights were cold, but he refused to come into the shelter, so I promised him a jacket. I promised to meet him the next day. But the night before, we had a water issue at the shelter, and I was up late trying to help fix it so the men could have hot showers in the morning. Later that afternoon, I went to the park to meet the guy who needed the jacket. I sat on the bench, and the warm sunshine made me feel drowsy. I laid down and closed my eyes for a moment. Ten minutes later, the guy showed up."

"So how was that trouble?"

"When Tori was helping Jake put together a fund-raiser for the Fatigues to Farming program, one of her friends had sent her pictures she'd taken of homeless men in the area, including one of me sleeping on the bench. I was worn out and filthy from working on the pipes. My brother thinks I was a homeless person sleeping on park benches."

"Why not tell him the truth?"

"I tried. The other day. But it doesn't matter. To Jake, I'm reckless and irresponsible, and nothing is going to change his opinion of me."

"But that's not who you are, so why would you allow him to continue to keep thinking that?"

"We live in a free country. He can think what he wants."

He sounded so bitter. Didn't he understand how lucky he was to have such a wonderful, supportive family? "Micah. That same freedom allows your pride to get in the way. You're just as stubborn as he is."

Micah pushed to his feet and held up his hand. "Listen, Paige, one thing I learned—we are not responsible for other people's thoughts and reactions. We're only responsible for our own. Jake will think what he wants, no matter what I say."

"Did you ever get in touch with your sister-in-law's photographer friend and demand that picture back?"

"Nope, not worth the hassle. I had more important things to take care of, such as doing what I could to help those men who had become homeless. I wanted to help them turn their lives around, to have a second chance at the life they deserved. I understood what they were going through. That feeling of hopelessness, that feeling of fear, of wondering where you were going to eat each day."

"But if you had come home, you could've had that here. From what I understand, your family created the Fatigues to Farming program with you in mind."

"It wasn't as simple as that. While I appreciate what my family has accomplished, none of them understands what it's like to lose a limb. Dad may have a better understanding with his back injury, but I know firsthand. And I can use that experience to help others overcome some of the struggles I endured so they can live their best lives."

"You're an inspiration, Micah." She stared at him, as if the intensity of her gaze could convince him.

"No, not even close. I'm just a guy who was stuck in the mud and was handed a shovel to dig his way out. Someone reached out and gave me a hand up. I want to do the same for others. Because of Phil and Ian, I had the break I needed to change. That's why it's important to stay on track with meeting our goals. A Hand

Up isn't a handout, but a second chance. Everyone deserves that. Now I can be the one to hand out a shovel."

"But your compassion helps change lives. That's evident by what you're doing here." She shrugged. "Who knows? Maybe God allowed you to go through everything you did so you'd be in a place to help someone else. Maybe you had to become homeless to understand their pain and give them the security they needed."

Micah laughed, the tone a bit raw and ragged. "Seems ironic that I had to lose an arm to give a hand up to others."

"I'm sorry for everything you've gone through." Paige reached for Micah's hand and gave it a squeeze. "God has a purpose for you. For this house. And for the men who will be living here." She tapped his chest. "And it started here. If you didn't care, you wouldn't have come home for Ian's funeral. You wouldn't be going through all this to get the transitional home set up. You wouldn't be talking to men like Jerome, encouraging them to take the next step."

And she wouldn't need to guard her heart to keep from falling for Micah. Because he was right—they needed to stay on track to meet their goals. And she couldn't lose sight of that, either, by doing something silly like falling for a man who had a hard time recognizing love in his own family.

Chapter Seven

Who would've thought they'd be flying kites in February?

But that was exactly how Micah convinced her they should take advantage of the gorgeous day with bright blue skies and sunshine radiating over them, turning the ice on the pond to a glittery frost.

To celebrate meeting their first milestone by launching a couple of Ian's kites.

After meeting that morning in Ginny's office, they learned they'd met the conditions for the first phase of receiving their inheritance. Phil Wilder, Dr. O'Brien and Ginny had approved their business plans, marketing proposals and renovation estimates. After receiving their checks for fifty grand, Micah insisted they take a break and celebrate.

While she might have preferred doing something inside, she had to admit bundling up and breathing in the crisp, fresh air while keeping her kite aloft did offer freedom from the hundreds of thoughts battering her brain.

Freedom from blueprints she didn't understand, cost estimates and whittling down her therapy wish list to align with her budget.

But at least she was making progress.

Her eyes swept across the yard to the tan metal building with the hunter-green roof that matched Micah's house. Turning the pole barn into her therapy center had been the perfect choice. With Grandpa helping with remodeling, she could cut some construction costs and divert those funds to her wish list items. And now that the brand-new fence had been installed, she didn't have to worry about escaping goats.

She'd had a virtual meeting with Dr. O'Brien last week to discuss the layout of the therapy center, then she and Grandpa met with the contractor who was helping to secure their permits needed for the renovations. Now that the insulation and drywall had been installed, she could begin painting this evening.

And with Tori putting together the open house, Paige had no doubt they'd get the money they needed to run their programs.

Finally, things were coming together.

So, yeah, maybe it was just fine to take a

break. To refresh her mind and to face the next phase with a positive perspective.

Tomorrow, she'd focus on the next thing.

For now, she'd try to keep her brightly colored dragonfly kite airborne.

"What are you scowling about? It's a beautiful day to be flying a kite."

Paige took her eyes off the single-line kite and looked at Micah, who did quite well controlling the line to his blue-and-orange box kite. "I'm wearing sunglasses, so how can you tell I'm scowling?"

"By the set of your jaw and your pressed lips. Not to mention that furrow between your eyebrows."

"I'm concentrating. Flying a kite in winter is hard work. Not to mention cold. I can't feel my nose."

"Good. For a moment I figured you were feeling guilty for taking the afternoon off when you could be learning more about raising goats, recalculating numbers or choosing paint colors for the tenth time."

It was like he could see inside her brain.

How did he maintain such an easy-breezy attitude and not let everything that still needed to be done weigh him down?

"There's still a lot that needs to be done."

"Of course, but it's okay to take a break, too.

In fact, it's necessary to avoid burning out before you even open your program."

"Just because I want to be prepared doesn't mean I'm headed toward burnout."

Micah reached her in two long-legged steps, set his reel on the ground, then slid her sunglasses up. He traced the curve below her eye. "And these dark shadows have nothing to do with a lack of sleep?"

She batted his hand away and settled her sunglasses back in place. "I can't help it—my brain doesn't turn off because it's bedtime."

"I've seen lights on in the barn as late as midnight and as early as four in the morning."

"I have a lot more responsibilities now. Besides, if you're seeing lights on, then you're not sleeping, either."

"It's not the same thing."

"How so?"

"I wake up and go back to sleep. You're surviving on a few hours of sleep. Your body and mind need more than that."

Paige's shoulders slumped. "There's so much to do. So much to learn."

"But it doesn't need to happen all at once."

"I need to keep ahead."

"Ahead of what? Your biggest competitor is you, Paige. Loosen up a little and enjoy the process."

"That's easy for you to say."

"Meaning?"

"In addition to working with clients, I'm trying to learn about goats and getting a therapy program up and running."

"How often have you asked for help?"

"Grandpa and Dr. O'Brien are helping me."

"Only because Ginny...well, Ian...mandated it."

She shot him a look. "I'm used to doing things on my own."

"You've said that a few times already, but why?"

Her mother's voice echoed from a memory she'd tucked away. *Figure it out, Paige. Can't you see I have more important things to do?*

"Because, as I've told you repeatedly—there's no one else." She fingered her heart necklace.

"But that's not true—you have your family, Dr. O'Brien, Natalie and Willow. And me."

She shook her head. He just didn't understand.

"My family is busy. Mom works full-time at the library, then spends her evenings and weekends caring for Abby. My grandparents are retired and deserve their downtime. Same with Dr. O'Brien. Nat's busy with her family, building her business and planning a wedding. Willow works long hours at the veterinarian clinic, then spends her free time with Julian. So, really, there is no one else." Paige's chest tightened.

Weren't they supposed to be celebrating?

The knot in Paige's throat grew as tears pressed against her eyes. Sniffing, she swallowed a couple of times and lifted her eyes to the cloudless bright blue sky.

Anything to keep from falling apart in the middle of the frozen pond.

Micah slid an arm around her shoulder. "I'm sorry for upsetting you. I didn't mean to make you cry."

She glared at him. "Cry? I'm not crying. I don't cry."

He brushed his thumb against her cheek and lifted it to show her. "If this isn't a tear, then your skin is leaking."

"Gross." She shook her head and slowly reeled in her kite.

"Paige, it's okay to let go, you know. You don't sleep. You don't cry. Or take time for yourself. Having such tight control isn't healthy."

"Control is a necessary part of my survival, Micah. Remember when my dad died a month after my thirteenth birthday?"

He nodded. "Yes, that freak accident at the red light, right?"

"Yes, he stopped at the light. The driver of the tractor trailer was distracted, didn't see the light turn and plowed into my dad's car, pushing him into the line of traffic. It was horrible."

"I remember."

"Well, what you might not know is my mom really struggled after his death. With working and caring for my sister, who was a toddler at the time and had just been diagnosed with CP, she didn't have a lot of time left for me. We ended up moving in with my grandparents. So, not only did I lose my dad, but I lost my room and all the memories of him in our house. At that time, my grandparents were still heavily involved in the ministry. They may have been away that week or something—I don't remember—but I do remember I struggled with an assignment and I'd asked Mom for help. She'd returned home early from work with my sister, who was sick. Anyway, she told me I needed to figure it out for myself because she had more pressing things to do. I admit it wasn't my best moment, but I fell apart."

"That's completely understandable."

"Not like that. I started yelling and crying, accusing her of never having time for me. She took me by my shoulders and told me I needed to pull myself together. I needed to be strong for her, because she was about to lose it."

"That's a lot to put on a kid."

Paige lifted a shoulder. "I realized I couldn't

ask for help. I needed to figure things out on my own. I needed to be the strong one. Because the last thing I wanted was to be the cause of my mother 'losing it.'" She air quoted the last two words.

"I'm sorry, Paige."

"There's nothing to be sorry for. I'm fine. From that moment on, I woke up early, made breakfast, made lunches for Abby and me, and helped my sister get ready for her childcare program. After school, I helped with housework, started supper, did my homework and helped Abby in any way I could."

"And when did you have time to be a kid?"

"I had Natalie and Willow as my friends. I didn't need anything else. I worked hard to get good grades so I could get a college scholarship. While in college, I worked two jobs to pay for my living expenses and education. I didn't ask anybody for anything."

Micah looked at her, his eyes soft and tender. "I'm sorry, Paige. I totally misjudged you. I thought you were this hyper workaholic who just wanted to compete with me."

She shook her head. "No, I needed to do my best to get money for college."

"Just so you know, I am always here for you. You can ask me for help for anything."

"That's sweet of you to say, Micah."

"And you have no plans to take me up on that, do you?"

She laughed. "Am I that transparent?"

"Let's just say, I understand not wanting to feel like a burden to others. But, Paige, you're not a kid anymore. It's okay to ask for help."

"Old habits run deep. Besides, I have asked you for help. Remember Buttons giving birth?"

"I was your last resort and you were panicking."

Her kite fluttered to the ground, and she leaned over to pick it up. "I'm getting hungry. If you really want to help, let's head back to the farm and check on the goats. Then we can make a batch of caramel corn and decide what to do next."

"Sounds like a plan to me."

What *was* next?

Not just for the program, but also for her and Micah.

She wanted to believe he was going to be there for her, but what if she started trusting and he walked away?

Holding on to her kite, she turned and stepped onto the bank. Her foot hit a patch of ice, and she slid. Dropping the kite, she reached out to break her fall as her weight fell on her right arm. Her shoulder rammed against the frozen ground as icy-hot pain sliced through her muscles. She let out a scream.

Micah whirled around, dropped his kite and hurried over to her. "What happened?"

"I slipped on a patch of ice, then landed on my shoulder." She pressed her right arm against her chest and rolled onto her back. The pulsing pain caused her stomach to churn.

"I'll help you stand, then we'll head to the ER to get your arm checked out." Micah crouched beside her. "Grab onto my shoulder, and I'll put my arm around you. Can you stand?"

"I hurt my arm, not my legs."

"Glad to hear you didn't lose that gentle tone."

"Sorry—I know you're trying to help. It just hurts."

"We'll get it taken care of."

"I planned to paint tonight. I guess that's out the window."

"I can help you with painting or whatever else you may need, so don't worry about that."

Easier said than done.

Sucking in a sharp breath, she allowed Micah to guide her to her feet, and then he helped her get buckled in the passenger seat. She pressed her head against the seat back and squeezed her eyes against the blur of tears and throbbing. Her to-do list scrolled rapidly through her head, and Paige wanted to crumple to the floor and weep.

One step forward, two steps back.

* * *

Micah shouldn't have pushed Paige into flying kites.

Honestly, he'd just wanted her to chill out a little and have some fun.

His great intentions had taken a wrong turn.

And now Paige had a sprained wrist and had injured the supraspinatus tendon in her right shoulder. With pain relievers and a course of steroids, it should heal fairly quickly as long as she didn't overdo it.

He knew she was suffering because of how she'd snapped at him at the emergency department, saying it was his fault. Yes, she'd immediately winced and apologized, but it was a mark of how much she hurt that she'd let that accusation pass her lips. He was learning how strong she was, but also how that strength could be tested.

He'd make it up to her by taking care of the goats, getting the painting done that she needed and whatever else he could to ensure her progress stayed on track.

Driving past her grandparents' house, he pulled into the driveway to the small cottage that sat on their property.

He grabbed the handled takeout bag out of the back seat, then followed the stone walk to the small white-sided cottage that looked like something from a kid's fairy tale.

He stepped onto the gray-painted porch, walked past the yellow rocking chair in the corner and rapped two knuckles against the door frame.

Barking came from the other side of the door.

"Just a minute," Paige called from inside.

Less than a minute later, she opened the door, her right arm in the sling from the emergency department. A small black-and-white blur shot past her legs and sniffed at Micah's feet. "Charlotte! Get back in here."

Micah crouched in front of the little bulldog and stroked her back. She rewarded him with a lick on the hand. Once she realized he wasn't going to hurt her, he scooped her up and set her on the floor inside the door. She raced into the room, stopped and watched him, her nubby tail wagging.

Paige wore a white T-shirt under an oversize knitted cardigan and a pair of navy yoga pants. "Micah. What are you doing here?"

"Can I come in?"

She shrugged, then winced. "I'm not in the best mood for company, so consider yourself warned."

"Duly noted." Grinning, he opened the screen

door and stepped inside, careful not to knock into her arm.

Micah glanced around the living room, taking in the painted beachscapes in tones of blue, green, gray and white hanging on the light gray walls with white trim. A navy couch sat under the window next to the entryway door with an oval coffee table in front of it. Across from the couch, a flat-screen TV sat above a lit electric fireplace, filling the room with a cozy warmth.

In the opposite corner, tall bookcases formed the backdrop for a matching navy chair with a paperback book turned upside down on its arm, along with a yellow afghan.

Paige closed the door behind him, revealing an antique secretary like the one his mom had in his parents' bedroom. A closed laptop and a pile of Ian's books about goats sat on the pull-down desk.

He stuffed his hand in his front pocket. "Nice place."

"Thanks." She headed toward the other end of the room. "When I was little, my great-grandparents lived here when they got older. After their deaths, my grandparents used the cottage to house visiting missionaries until my grandpa retired from the pulpit. Once I graduated college, I moved in here. I have my own space but I'm still close enough to help Mom, Abby and

Grandma and Grandpa. Come into the kitchen with me. I'm trying to make some tea."

Noticing her socked feet, Micah toed off his slip-on loafers, leaving them next to the Hello, Winter floor mat decorated with snowflakes, which caused him to grin even wider, and followed her into the kitchen painted the same gray and white as the living room.

"Let me help." He set the bag on the table, then reached for the kettle she was trying to pour with her left hand.

"I can handle it. The last thing we need is another accident."

One side of his mouth lifted at her sassy attitude. "Oh, get over yourself, Paige. You were having a great time until you got hurt."

"Sure, but it's going to be tough to get walls painted and tend to goats and help my clients with my arm in a sling."

"Thankfully, the injury is minor and will heal quickly, so you'll be back to your independent self in no time. In the meantime, I'll help with anything you need. We're partners, remember?"

"What do you know about setting up a therapy center?"

"Paige, you hurt your arm, not your brain." He flexed his arm. "Consider me your muscle. Now stop feeling sorry for yourself and tell me how to help."

Gripping the edge of the counter with her good hand, she dropped her chin to her chest and released a sigh. "I'm sorry. I haven't slept well. The pain's making me cranky."

"You don't say."

She shot him a dirty look. "Would you like some tea?"

"No, thanks. Why don't you sit and I will get it for you?"

She moved to the small table, pulled out one of the chairs and sat. She cradled her forehead in her hand. "The tea is in the round canister on the counter. The cups are in the cabinet above it."

Micah opened the cabinet and reached for a white mug decorated with a goat that read You've Goat to Be Kidding Me. He grinned. "Cute cup."

"My last Christmas present from Ian."

Micah dropped a tea bag into the cup, then carried it to the table. He reached for the steaming kettle on the stove and filled the mug. "Need milk or sugar?"

"Just milk."

After she added milk to her tea, Micah returned the carton to the fridge. He reached for the bag he'd set on the table and pulled out the bouquet of mixed blossoms in pinks, purples and yellows, then handed them to her. "I thought these might brighten your day."

She took them and buried her nose in the petals. "Thank you, Micah. I can't remember the last time anyone gave me flowers."

Shame.

She deserved to be appreciated.

He set the bag on the empty chair across from her and pulled out a bakery box, then a recyclable takeout box. "I wasn't sure if you'd eaten or not, so I stopped at Cuppa Josie's to grab a couple of cinnamon rolls, then I picked up a club sandwich and fries from Joe's Diner. But if you're not hungry, you can always save it for later."

"Mom invited me for dinner, but I told her I was too tired to go. I figured I'd eat cereal and call it good."

Spying a glass turned upside down on the drying mat next to her sink, Micah filled it with water then leaned against the counter. "I'll feed and water the goats. I can get Evan to give me a hand with deworming, trimming hooves or whatever else needs to be done. Just tell me what to do. He and I can begin painting for you, too. I'm sure Natalie will lend a hand as well."

She waved away his words. "No, don't ask them. Their wedding is coming up, and Nat's so busy already with the kennels and their dog fostering program. I'll take care of what needs to be done."

"Do you know how annoying that answer is becoming? Why are you being so stubborn? I'm offering to help, but you're blowing me off because of your ridiculous pride." He smiled to take the sting out of his words, but he was tired of the double standard.

Paige looked at him a moment, then her face crumpled. Shaking her head, she covered her face with her hand, but it did little to silence the messy sobs through her fingers.

Micah's eyes widened. *Oh, great.*

He didn't see Paige cry very often. And knowing he was the reason didn't leave a good feeling in his gut.

Setting the glass on the counter, he grabbed a dish towel and knelt in front of her. He slid his arm around her and set the towel on her lap. "Hey, I'm sorry."

She mopped her eyes, then exhaled as her chest shuddered. "I'm sorry. I'm just so tired. I feel like the past few weeks have been a nonstop marathon, and I'm coming in last place."

"What are you talking about? We just met our first milestone. You're a champion, Paige."

"Yes, but I've also done it while still working with my remote clients, caring for the goats and helping Abby as much as possible."

"While you're taking care of everyone else, who is taking care of you?"

She dropped her hands in her lap and lowered her head, shaking it slightly. "There is no one."

Micah cupped her chin and forced her to look at him. "Like I've been saying all along, I'm here for you. You have to choose to believe it. We'll get through this together."

"Why are you helping me?"

"I'm your friend. Drink your tea, then you can take a nap."

"I still have so much to do today."

"Your to-do list can wait until tomorrow. So eat something, finish your tea and then take some medicine."

She nodded and reached for her cup.

He found a plate and added half the sandwich and fries, then set it in front of her. "I'll put the other half in the fridge so you can eat it later."

She shook her head. "Fries aren't very good once they've gotten cold and then have been reheated. Why don't you join me and eat it instead?"

Micah carried the takeout container over to the table and sat across from her. She mumbled a quiet prayer, then they ate their sandwiches.

After they'd finished eating, Micah carried the dishes to the sink and threw away the trash. Quickly, he washed her cup and plate and set them on the drying mat. Then he moved over to the table and touched her elbow. "Let's get you into the living room so you can rest."

Paige settled on the couch, laid back against the pillow, closed her eyes and released a sigh as she cradled her arm.

Micah grabbed one of the throw pillows at the other end of the couch and tucked it under her arm.

She sucked in a sharp breath.

He shot her a look. "Sorry. Just trying to keep it stable."

She waved away his apology. "It's fine."

He reached for the yellow knitted afghan and draped it over her. Then he sat on the edge of the cushion beside her. Charlotte pawed at his leg. He lifted her up and settled her on the end of the couch away from Paige's injured arm.

Her eyelids fluttered as she fought to stay awake.

Micah brushed her hair away from her face. "Would you like me to stay in case you need anything?" He held his breath, hoping she'd say yes. He wanted to take care of her, to show her how easy it was to accept help when in need.

She reached for his hand and gave it a gentle squeeze. "You've done enough. Thank you. For everything. And I am sorry. This is not your fault. I was upset and lashed out at you."

He lifted his shoulder. "No big deal. I can take

it. You get some sleep, and I'll text you later to see how you're feeling. Where's your phone?"

She pointed to the coffee table in front of the couch. "Right there."

"Is it charged?"

She shrugged, then winced. "Maybe. Honestly, I haven't really checked."

"Where's your charger? I'll plug it in for you."

"It's no big deal, Micah. I'll be fine."

He bit back a laugh. Her reflexive first response was always to refuse help. "No. You always need to have a charged phone."

He found the charging cord, plugged in her phone and then set it back on the coffee table. He knelt in front of her and longed to press a comforting kiss against her forehead, but he didn't want to risk upsetting her any more than necessary.

His eyes roamed over her face, taking in her fair complexion, the smattering of light freckles she chose to cover most days with makeup and her blue eyes that reminded him of summertime. She was the most beautiful woman he'd ever seen. Yet she didn't realize just how much.

"Stop staring at me. You're making me nervous." Her eyes remained closed as her words slurred from fatigue.

Laughing softly and despite his longing to stay where he was, Micah pushed to his feet and readjusted the blanket over her. He caressed her cheek. "Get some rest, Sleeping Beauty. I'll check on you later."

She nodded, then once her breathing settled into a steady, rhythmic pattern, Micah let himself out of the cottage quietly so he didn't disturb her.

A plan formed in his head as he considered showing Paige just how good they could be together.

Not just as business partners, but also with each other.

Chapter Eight

Paige needed to pull it together.

It was just lunch after church to say thank you. No need to read any more into it than that.

After all, she'd spent more time with Micah over the past few weeks than she had in the past eight years, and they were both still standing.

So inviting him to the cottage for one meal was not a big deal.

But that was the thing—it wasn't *just* one meal.

They were having lunch with Mom and Abby.

Micah's care and compassion for her since her injury made her realize something very scary—she was falling for her childhood frenemy. He'd not only helped her after the accident. He'd put up with her snarky moods, her snappish attitude. Even though she wasn't used to accepting help, he gave it in spite of her resistance. That's when she really started thinking maybe they could be more than friends.

And if he could be a part of her life, then she needed to see how he interacted with her mom and her sister.

And the fact that Micah had said yes to coming, well, that filled her with something else she wasn't quite ready to name.

So for now she needed to focus on lunch.

The timer dinged on the stove. She reached for pot holders, then pulled a blackberry pie out of the oven. Using her left hand was a little awkward, but she managed to set it on the stove top next to the baked pasta without dropping it or burning herself.

The scents of baked sugar blending with the aroma of Italian seasoning and marinara sauce made her anxious stomach growl.

A light tapping sounded on her front door.

She dropped the pot holders on the counter and headed for the living room, pausing for half a second to glance in the mirror by the door to check her appearance. Then she made a face at her reflection.

Stop it.

It was just Micah.

So what was up with the sudden fluttering in her stomach?

She exhaled, then opened the door.

Micah stood on her front mat dressed in a charcoal-colored sweater and the jeans she'd seen him wearing at church that morning. His dark, wavy hair glossed under the sunlight. He held a gift bag in his hand.

"Hey. Come in." Holding on to the door, Paige stepped back and waved him in. As he passed, she breathed in the scent of his soap. He smelled like fresh air and sunshine with a hint of something spicy. "I'm glad you could make it. My mother and my sister are sitting on the sunporch."

"How are you feeling?"

Paige lifted a shoulder. "The meds are helping with the inflammation and pain. It's awkward to have the use of only one arm, though."

"Yeah, tell me about it." His rich laughter bounced around the room.

Paige's face heated at her faux pas. "Sorry. That was insensitive."

"Paige, stop. I'm well aware of my limitations. Thankfully, yours are temporary."

She waved toward the kitchen. "I'll take you to the sunporch, then I'll come back for the food."

"Need a hand?" A half smile slid across his face. "That's all I have to offer anyway."

She rolled her eyes at him. "Aren't you getting tired of that joke?"

He lifted a shoulder. "Sometimes I have to make a joke to ease the tension."

"Tension? What tension?" Her voice squeaked on the last syllable.

His half smile turned into a wide-mouthed grin. "Sorry, my mistake."

Shaking her head, she led him to where her family sat. "Mom, Abby, Micah's here."

Stepping out onto the enclosed porch, Micah held out his hand to her mother. "Nice to see you again, Mrs. Watson."

"Micah Holland, I've known you since you were in diapers. What's this handshake business? Give me a hug and call me Wendy."

"Yes, ma'am." Micah hugged her, then he crouched in front of Abby's wheelchair. He handed her the pink gift bag. "Hey, Abby. Paige said you like music. When I was cleaning out Ian's attic, I found this and thought you might like it."

"Hi, Micah." Smiling at him, Abby reached into the bag and pulled out a small wooden box with a kite carved on the top. "Oh, it's so pretty."

Micah stretched out his hand. "May I?"

She nodded.

Very gently, Micah turned over the box, and Abby gasped when she saw the key. "It's a music box." She gave it a few turns.

She closed her eyes and moved her head in

time to the music as she hummed along. Then she opened her eyes and smiled. "It's playing 'Let's Go Fly a Kite' from *Mary Poppins*."

"Yes, and not only that, but I think Ian made it for Betsy. If you open the lid, you will see something special inside."

Abby opened the lid and read, "'To my favorite kite-flying partner. My love for you soars higher and higher each day. Yours, Ian.'" She traced her finger over the engraved words, then threw her arms around his neck. "Thank you, Micah. This is the best gift."

"You're welcome."

"Will you sit beside me for lunch?"

He reached for her small hand and gave it a squeeze. "It would be my pleasure."

"Would you like to see my music box collection?"

He exchanged looks with Paige, then returned his attention to Abby. "You collect music boxes?"

She nodded. "I thought Paige told you. That's why you gave it to me."

Micah shook his head. "No, I gave it to you because of the music. Knowing you collect music boxes makes me so glad I chose the right gift."

She lowered her eyes and traced the outline

of the carved kite with a shaky finger. "I miss Ian and Betsy."

"Me, too. This way, you have a small piece of them with you always."

Eyes warming and needing a little breathing space from the sweet Hallmark moment on the sunporch, Paige returned to the kitchen for the casserole.

Sliding a folded dish towel under the warm pan to balance on her left arm, she lifted it off the stove, then turned and nearly ran into Micah. The dish teetered.

Micah palmed the bottom of the pan to steady it, his large hand covering hers.

Paige sucked in a breath, then exhaled slowly. "Thanks. I didn't hear you come in."

"I have the skills of a ninja." The subtle lines around his eyes deepened as he grinned.

She laughed, wishing—not wishing—he'd let go. "Apparently so."

Over his shoulder, she glanced at her sister, turning the key once again on the music box. "That was a very sweet gift you gave Abby. Thank you."

"Actually, I set it aside for you until you mentioned she liked music."

"She'll cherish it." Paige nodded toward the pan they still held. "I need to get this on the table so we can eat."

"Need me to carry anything?"

She jerked her head toward the glass bowl on the counter. "Grab the salad, please."

Finally releasing his hold on the pasta dish, Micah picked up the salad and followed her out the door.

Once they had been seated and the food blessed, they filled their plates and started eating.

Abby's sweet laughter and the relaxing of Mom's shoulders as Micah shared funny stories from his childhood showed Paige how well Micah could fit into their lives.

She had worried for nothing.

Or maybe she knew that and was looking for a reason to keep him at arm's length? Because if she didn't, she'd have to risk her heart to possible pain and heartbreak when he walked away.

Seeing how gentle and compassionate Micah was with her sister made Paige realize she was a goner, and she'd have to work harder to keep her feelings to herself. The true test of character for her was how someone treated Abby. And Micah continued to give Abby his full attention as she went into great detail about her music box collection, waiting patiently for her to speak. Not to mention he couldn't have chosen a better gift.

However, she still found herself mentally pulling away in order to protect herself and their working relationship. Nothing ruined a partnership faster than a personal interest in each other. And she had no idea if he considered her more than a partner or if he was just showing his true, caring self.

Somehow, she had to figure out how to keep her growing feelings for Micah from getting in the way of her goals.

Once they had finished eating, Mom helped her clear the table while Micah and Abby stayed on the sunporch.

Mom scraped the plates, then loaded them into the compact dishwasher while Paige cut and plated the blackberry pie. They carried dessert back to the table.

After finishing the last bite, she closed her eyes, leaned back in her chair and folded her hands over her very full stomach. Afternoon sunshine streamed in through the floor-to-ceiling windows and lulled Paige into a drowsy state of contentment. She could get used to the male laughter at her table, having someone to lend a hand. Someone to lean on.

What would that be like?

"Looks like you could use a nap."

Paige's eyes flew open to find Micah standing over her. "Nah. Just enjoying the sunshine… and the company."

His eyes darkened as a smile slid in place. "Thank you for a wonderful afternoon, but I need to head out."

Paige slid back her chair and walked Micah to the front door. "Thank you for coming."

He reached for her left hand and gave it a gentle squeeze. His eyes drifted over her shoulder, then back to her face. "Thanks for lunch. It was great. See you later?"

She nodded and pocketed her hands so she wouldn't throw her arms around his neck.

After Micah backed out of the driveway, Paige returned to the patio, stacked the pie plates and carried them into the kitchen.

"You like him." Her mom pressed her back against the sink, dishcloth in her hand.

Paige added the plates to the dishwasher, then started it. Taking the dishcloth from her mother, she wiped down the counter. "Of course I like him. I've known him all my life."

"I'm not talking about friendship, Paige."

Paige paused a moment, her eyes focused on a spot of dried sauce on the stove. "Mom, Micah and I are partners."

Mom placed a hand on Paige's back. "I know. That's why I worry. You'll be together a lot. I don't want you setting yourself up for heartbreak. Or risking losing sight of your goals."

"That's not going to happen. Micah and I need to stay on task so we can meet our deadlines. We've fallen into a rhythm of working well together. Honestly, who has time for romance anyway?"

"Honey, I just don't want to see you get hurt."

"I appreciate that, but I'm a grown woman who can take care of herself." Paige balled up the dishcloth and tossed it into the sink, banking it off the faucet.

"You've always been so independent." Mom tucked a stray piece of Paige's hair behind her ear.

Not always by choice.

Paige grabbed Mom's hand. "I appreciate your concern, but you're worrying for nothing. Micah and I are friends, working together to put our programs in place." Maybe if she said it enough, she'd believe it, too.

"If you say so. I just want you to be careful."

"Seriously? Careful is my middle name."

Problem was, the more time she spent with Micah, the less careful she wanted to be.

What would it be like to take that leap of faith and risk her heart with a guy who could potentially give her everything she'd always wanted?

Or would she simply be setting herself up for heartbreak, like her mother warned?

Was it worth the risk to find out?

* * *

Just when he thought he had a leg up, Micah had things coming down around his ears. What was he going to do now?

Somehow, he needed to figure out how to move forward with the house renovations on his own.

After discovering some of the construction crew had been using inferior materials instead of what had been quoted, Micah had confronted Lefty about cutting corners, which led to a very vocal argument about safety and compliance. When Micah threatened legal action, Lefty and his guys walked off the job, leaving Micah with a lot that still needed to be done and little time to do it.

He was wasting time feeling sorry for himself.

Micah shoved to his feet, opened the newly installed automatic door and headed back inside the house that smelled of sawdust and paint fumes.

Any other day, those scents would've pleased Micah. But today they just reminded him of how much he couldn't do on his own.

The kitchen with the newly added exposed wood beams had been remodeled to Paige's specifications. Ian's cabinets had been sanded down and restained a light oak with pullout drawers instead of shelves. An unobstructed sink and cooktop had been installed. They had removed the scarred table and added a lower peninsula off the main counters for wheelchair accessibility. The worn linoleum had been replaced with laminate wood flooring.

Micah walked into the living room that remained untouched, but it needed nothing more than a good cleaning and a paint job. Thankfully, the archway to this room was wide enough already and didn't need further renovations. By removing most of the furniture, there'd be enough clearance.

However, the bathrooms had been next on the renovation list, and none of those had been touched. Lefty had ordered a large roll-in shower for the downstairs bathroom. The box sat in the hall, waiting to be installed.

The two downstairs bedrooms still needed doorways widened.

So much yet to be done in two weeks.

The front door opened. "Yo, Micah. Are you in here?"

Micah strode down the hall to the front door to find Evan, dressed in a green sweatshirt and tan cargo shorts despite the low temps, standing in the entryway. "Hey, man. What's going on?"

"You ready to go?"

"Go? Where?"

Evan jerked a thumb out the door. "Remember? You were going to the fitness center with me to test out different adaptive kayaks in the pool."

Micah banged the heel of his hand against his forehead. "Oh, that's right. Sorry, it slipped my mind."

"You okay?"

Micah shook his head. "No, not really."

"What's going on? Problems with Paige?"

"No. For once, she's the only thing working out right now. My contractor and his crew walked off the job."

Evan pulled off his sunglasses. "What? Why?"

"Lefty's guys were cutting corners with inferior materials, and when I called them on it, they bailed. Now I have two weeks to pull this house together without a crew."

Evan jerked a thumb toward the driveway. "Jake's waiting in the truck. I'll let him know what's going on, and we'll figure something out together."

Great. Once again, Micah the Menace needed to be bailed out.

Micah hesitated, then followed his brother out the door. If Jake was going to say anything about him, Micah wanted to hear it.

Jake stepped out of the truck and leaned on the open door. "Heard you had some trouble."

"Something like that."

"We may have a solution." Evan exchanged a look with Jake.

Micah rested an elbow on the hood. "What kind of solution?"

"Jake suggested I get a hold of Preacher, one of my former kayaking teammates, and see if we can get the crew up here to lend a hand."

"I appreciate it, but don't those guys have jobs?"

Evan grinned. "Well, Preacher owns a construction company and has various crews working for him."

Micah straightened as a flicker of hope ignited in his chest. "No way. Do you think he'll come up?"

Evan shrugged, pulled out his phone, and waved it. "Only one way to find out."

Micah looked at Jake. "Thanks, man."

"Any time, little brother. Hop in. We'll grab some tacos from Lena's food truck. Then we can head back to the farmhouse and hash this out with Dad. Tuck should be off duty soon, so he can join us."

"Mind if I invite Paige? This impacts her, too."

"Not at all." Jake grinned.

An hour later, the noise level at the Holland farmhouse rose to the point where Micah gave up trying to hear all the different conversations. The dining room table was covered in tacos, carnitas, enchiladas and burritos, and plenty of chips and salsa.

Being surrounded by his brothers and their families, Micah was feeling like the odd man out once again.

The doorbell rang, but he would be surprised if anyone else heard it above the noise. Being closest to the door, he opened it to find Paige standing on the welcome mat wearing jeans, brown leather boots that came to her knees, a soft pink sweater that highlighted the color in her cheeks, and her fur-trimmed parka. "You made it."

She stepped inside. "Thanks for inviting me. You said there was something we needed to talk about?" She winced at the noise of laughter and loud conversation. "You sure you want to talk about it here?"

Grabbing his leather jacket off a hook by the door, Micah jerked his head toward the porch. "Let's go outside."

They stepped through the door, and he closed it behind them, shutting out the commotion. Micah sat on the porch swing, then patted the empty spot beside him. "Have a seat for a minute."

Paige sat next to him and burrowed her chin

deeper into her zipped jacket. "We have an audience."

Micah looked up to see his brothers standing in front of the window watching them while shoving tacos in their mouths. Scowling, he waved them away. Their laughter echoed through the glass as they turned their backs to them. "No privacy around here."

"So what did you want to talk to me about?"

Micah told Paige about his confrontation with Lefty.

Paige slowed the swing with her foot and stood. Arms wrapped around her waist, she paced in front of the door. "We have two weeks before the next deadline."

Micah rose and stopped the swing to keep it from hitting him in the back of his legs. He stood in front of Paige and pressed a hand on her shoulder. "We may have a solution to our problem."

"What's that?"

"One of Evan's former teammates has his own construction company. Evan put a call into Preacher, and hopefully he can come up to lend a hand."

"I've met Preacher. He's a good guy." Paige waved a hand toward the dining room window. "So that's what this is?"

"Yeah, I guess. Jake, Evan and I were supposed to test out adaptive kayaks at the pool, but with what happened with Lefty and his crew, we decided to grab some food and head back here to figure things out. I wanted you to be included. Well, it's turned into a noisy family gathering."

"Those are the best kind." She shot him a sweet smile that melted his heart and reached for his hand. "Thanks for including me. Let's grab some tacos before your brothers devour them all."

Micah opened the door for her. Inside, they filled their plates, then joined the others in the living room.

His father sat next to Micah on the sectional. "You okay?"

Micah pulled out his phone and thumbed through the photos he'd taken before his brothers arrived. "I'm questioning the quality of the work that's been done already. How do I know if it's even up to code? They broke my trust. So much work needs to be done. They haven't even touched the upstairs, but at least most of that is cosmetic. But…" The weight of his to-do list pressed on Micah's shoulders. Resting his elbow on his knee, he cupped his forehead. "Man, this is such a mess."

His dad clamped a hand on his shoulder. "Deep breath, son. We'll pull together and get it all worked out."

"Thanks, Pops."

Evan pulled out his phone, read something on the screen, then gave a whoop that caused Charlie to let out a wail. Evan grimaced, then shot an apologetic look at Tori, who was trying to soothe her son. "Sorry, little dude." He looked at Micah. "Preach will be here tomorrow. He and a couple of his guys will do a walk-through with you, then determine the next steps to take." Evan turned and waved his hand over the family. "We'll help in any way we can. Lefty may think he's left you high and dry, but he doesn't realize what Holland Strong really means."

Micah dropped his gaze to the floor and swallowed past the thickening in his throat.

Apparently, he had forgotten, too.

His eyes roamed over the tattoo, peeking from beneath his pulled up T-shirt sleeve, inked on the inside of his forearm, of the solid oak tree with each of his brothers' names written in the roots. He and his brothers did have roots that ran deep. Despite the trials each one of them faced, they were there for one another.

Something he needed to start remembering.

His phone vibrated in his back pocket. He pulled it out to find Phil's face on the screen. "Hey, Phil. What's going on?"

"Micah, I'm sorry to be the bearer of bad news, but Jerome's been taken to the hospital."

"Hospital? What's going on?"

"He overdosed."

"What? When?" Ice slid through his veins. He turned away from his family watching him. Pressure mounted behind his eyes. He swallowed several times. "Is he... Will he make it?"

"Too soon to tell, but I hope so. I need to call his family."

"No, I'll do it. I'm leaving now. I'll be down in about three and a half hours." Micah ended the call. "I have to go. There's an emergency with one of the guys at the Next Step."

"What about Preach?"

Micah's eyes bounced from Evan to Paige. "You know my plans. We've talked through everything. Will you meet with Preach?"

Paige set her plate on the end table and stood, placing a hand on his arm. "Yes, of course. Whatever you need. Are you okay?"

He shook his head, then pressed a kiss to her cheek and squeezed her hand. "Thanks, Paige. You're the best. I'm really sorry, but I need to go."

As Micah headed for the front door, his father stepped in front of him. "What can we do?"

"Pray." Micah hurried outside, searched for his SUV, then remembered he'd ridden to the farm with his brothers. He jogged down the driveway, then sprinted down the road to Ian's place, reciting the same prayer with each footfall. "God, please save him."

Chapter Nine

Micah had failed.

His goal had been to get his program going and bring some of the guys like Jerome up from the city and offer them a fresh start. They just needed to hold on a little longer.

It wasn't supposed to be like this. He shouldn't have had to attend his second funeral in just a handful of weeks.

The heaviness against his ribs lessened slightly as his property came into view.

And he saw Paige's car parked by the barn.

Instead of pulling into his driveway, he drove past his house and parked next to her car.

He gripped the steering wheel, then blew out a breath before exiting the vehicle.

Paige appeared in the doorway, and it was all he could do to keep from running to her and wrapping her in his embrace. Instead, he lifted his hand and gave a little wave. "Hey."

Without a word, she opened her arms. His chest heaved. He walked into them, wrapped his arm around her waist and buried his face into her shoulder, breathing in the floral scent of her shampoo.

"Natalie told me about your friend. I'm so sorry for your loss." Her words whispered against his ear.

His eyes filmed as the knot in his throat tightened. All he could do was nod without sobbing into her hair.

He drew back, tipped her chin and searched her blue eyes. He lowered his head slowly and brushed a soft kiss across her lips. Her hands cradled his face as she returned the kiss. Micah tightened his hold on her, not wanting to let her go.

Her fingers slid into his hair as she slowed the kiss, then pressed her cheek to his chest.

He rested his chin on the top of her head as he willed his racing heart to return to its regular rhythm. Whatever that was when Paige was around.

"Welcome home." Her words were muffled against the cotton fabric of his T-shirt.

Two little words.

Yet they were the best ones he'd heard in a while.

"If I'd known that was going to be my welcome, I would have left sooner." He grinned as her cheeks reddened.

She stroked a thumb over his cheekbone, her eyes bright and a smile tugging at her lips. "What am I going to do with you?"

He had a few ideas. He shrugged. "Just hug me, I guess."

"I can do that." She slid her arms around his waist and rested her head against his chest again. "I missed you. I'm glad you're home."

"Me, too."

Home.

Another word that filled him with warmth. He hadn't had a real home since he left the farm to enlist.

And now he didn't want to leave again unless Paige was at his side.

As her fingers tightened around his back, Micah finally admitted what he'd been too afraid to face—he was in love with Paige.

And he had no idea what to do about it. But for now, he simply enjoyed the moment.

In her embrace, he felt forgiven, as if all the mistakes of his past were wiped away. He felt whole, whatever the shape of his body. He felt understood and cherished.

"Wanna talk about it?"

Micah released her, then slipped his hand in hers. He ran his thumb over her soft skin. "Jerome came to the Next Step before Thanksgiving. I'd met him on the streets and finally convinced him to give Phil's program a try. His anger issues and subsequent drug abuse caused his wife to leave, taking their two kids with her. He couldn't keep a job and lost his apartment, rendering him homeless. When he came to Phil's, his main goal was to get his wife and kids back. So he got clean, started attending a recovery program, got involved in Phil's church and really started to turn a corner. Apparently, his wife filed for divorce last month—that's when he called me. He'd just learned his wife wants to marry someone else. He spiraled, undoing so much of the great work he had done. We tried to encourage him and help him through the pain and loss, but…" Micah dragged a hand over his face. "We weren't enough. He overdosed on pain pills. They rushed him to the hospital, but he died an hour later."

"I'm so sorry."

"Yeah, me too. I was too late. I couldn't save him."

"Oh, sweetie, it wasn't your job to save him. Only God could have done that. But what you're doing is good and right. And it will help someone else get the hand up they need." Paige cupped his face. "Don't blame yourself for this. We have different programs, but we have similar goals—we want the best for those who go through our programs."

"I know. And you're right. By working together, we can make it happen." He cradled her hand against his chest.

She smiled, but the light in her eyes dimmed. He frowned. "What's wrong?"

"Preach was on his way up yesterday, but he had to turn around. His wife was in a serious car accident."

"Oh, no! Is she okay?"

Paige nodded. "I think so. Evan drove down yesterday to see if he could do anything to help. Natalie called me last night and said Tasha had broken her clavicle. Preach needs to be home to care for their kids while his wife recovers."

"I'm so sorry to hear that. And I know this is very selfish in light of what happened, but I don't know what to do now." Micah stepped away from Paige and dragged his hand over his weary face. "Even if I had two arms, I still couldn't do the remodel myself in such a short amount of time. I can fix things, but I'm not skilled in home renovation."

"Your family built the cabins for the Fatigues

to Farming program. Maybe they will be able to help you out."

"They're so busy with the program, the farm and their own lives. I can't ask them to do more."

"Can't or won't?"

"What are you talking about?"

"You've been preaching to me about being willing to ask for help, but you don't take your own advice."

"That's different."

"How so?"

"No one pities you." And she didn't have brothers like his—or at least Jake—who judged him lacking. Asking for more of their help would just confirm their poor opinion of his abilities.

"Are you sure you're not viewing your family's willingness to lend a hand through a clouded lens?"

"Man, it feels like we are fighting a losing battle. One step forward, two steps back. What was Ian thinking? I was content with being in Pittsburgh and helping Phil."

"Maybe Ian saw something in you and knew you were destined for more."

Micah scoffed. "I doubt that."

"You know, Micah, until you get out of your own way, you won't be able to see yourself as others do."

"What's that supposed to mean?"

"Describe yourself to me in two words. An adjective and a noun."

"What? That's ridiculous. I'm not doing that." As much as he admired Paige's compassion, he wasn't up to a counseling session with her. He'd been through enough of those already.

"Why? Are you afraid?"

He rolled his eyes, kicked the toe of his boot into the corner of the goat pen, then glared at Paige. "Scarred amputee. Happy?"

She folded her arms over her chest and matched his glare with her own. "Very. It tells me you're hung up on your physical appearance and you try to hide it from the world rather than seeing yourself as others see you. As God sees you."

"Oh, yeah? How do you think He sees me?"

"A redeemed son, Micah. Instead of looking at offers of help as being given out of pity, clear your vision and embrace the blessing of people wanting to be a part of your ministry. When you allow people to see how God is working in your life…" She waved a hand over the property. "You're giving Him the glory. And that's the story people need to hear. Not that you are a scarred amputee but that you are redeemed and working hard to empower others to share their stories, too. Step out of the shadows of your past and allow God to shine His light on your future."

He searched her face, and the compassion that radiated from her eyes nearly buckled his knees.

For the last four years, he'd hidden behind the labels placed on him after his injury. How was he supposed to change that thinking in an instant?

He didn't know the answer, but he did know one thing—his story wouldn't be complete unless Paige continued to be a part of it, because she was the one person who saw beyond the scars and into his heart.

The one person who could give him the life he'd always wanted.

Paige liked being right, but now it came with a price.

Sure, Micah had listened to her and asked his family for help. And yes, as she'd expected, they were quick to jump in and do what needed to be done. But as the deadline loomed closer, the grumpier Micah had become.

And if he bit her head off one more time over something stupid, she was going to send one of her goats after him.

After all, she had her own issues to deal with, too.

Yes, ensuring his renovations met compliance was important, but no different than starting her therapy program. Now that the interior rooms had been divided and drywalled, she needed to finish painting so she could get the therapy equipment in place and sensory spaces set up. Not to mention finding time to conduct interviews for office administration and an occupational therapy assistant, for starters.

If her business picked up, she could consider hiring another therapist.

If the partnership with Micah's transitional home worked out, then she wouldn't have to worry about barn chores.

She had to admit she wouldn't mind giving up the feeding and cleaning up the barns every day.

How had Ian done everything by himself for so long?

He wasn't trying to juggle caring for the goats with working full-time by doing in-home therapies with the clients she'd kept after Dr. O'Brien closed his practice, she reminded herself.

Her early mornings and late nights were beginning to take their toll, but it would be worth it once they achieved their goals.

She just needed to keep her eyes on the prize.

But she was tired.

She shouldn't be lifting the pitchfork until her wrist and shoulder were fully healed, but a farmer's work didn't stop with mild injuries.

Paige leaned the pitchfork against the stall and rubbed her hand over the back of her neck, trying to ease the knotted muscles at the top of her spine.

Her fingers stilled.

Wait a minute. Where'd her necklace go?

Paige dropped to the dirty floor and sifted through loose hay, scraping her hands through bedding and debris as she searched for even a glint of shiny metal. She'd been so busy cleaning she hadn't realized the necklace was missing. Now it could be anywhere.

But apparently not in the barn.

She squeezed her eyes shut and mentally retraced her steps. Her alarm had gone off at 4:00 a.m. She remembered seeing her necklace around her neck when she'd looked in the mirror to brush her teeth and pull her hair into a ponytail.

Sitting back on her feet, she eyed the wheelbarrow full of used bedding and goat manure.

Ugh.

The thought of digging through that muck… Was it even worth it?

Pushing to her feet, she moved to the wheelbarrow. She pulled on a pair of work gloves and, wrinkling her nose, she dug slowly through the bedding and hay. Maybe it would be easier to find if she dumped the wheelbarrow contents on the floor and spread it around.

But this wasn't her first wheelbarrow load

since she arrived at the barn at four thirty. Her shoulders sagged at the thought of having to dig through the goat compost pile behind the barn.

"Paige? Are you in here?" The threads around Micah's voice sounded frayed.

"In here." She sat on the floor and curled her feet under her as she dug through the contents of the wheelbarrow once more.

"What are you doing?"

She looked over her shoulder. Micah stood in the doorway wearing worn jeans and a red-and-blue-plaid flannel shirt opened over a navy T-shirt that clung to him like a second skin. She turned her attention back to the debris on the floor, needing to focus on her task at hand and not Micah's sculpted muscles. "I lost my necklace."

"The heart one you always wear?"

She nodded, struggling to push words past the lump in her throat. "I had it when I came to the barn, and now it's gone."

"Let's retrace your steps. Start from leaving your house."

"I got in my car and drove to the barn. I came inside and rinsed out all the water buckets and refilled them. Then I refilled the food buckets with grain. I sat on the bench and played with Lulu and Daffy for about ten minutes. Once the goats finished eating, I let them out into the pasture, then I started cleaning stalls, filling the wheelbarrow full of used bedding and hay. I emptied one wheelbarrow into the compost pile behind the barn. I was halfway through the last stall when I realized my necklace was missing."

Micah crouched beside her and took her elbow. "Let's go back to your car and see if it came off out there. Then we'll do a walk-through. If we can't find it, I'll dig through the compost pile."

She brushed the back of her gloved hand across her forehead, the fatigue draining her. "Why would you do that for me?"

Micah ran a thumb over her cheek. "Because it's important to you. And you're important to me. Since it's obviously so special, I want to help you find it."

"My dad gave it to me for my thirteenth birth-day...a month before he was killed." She pressed a hand against her bare throat.

Micah pressed his lips against her forehead. "I'm sorry, Paige. We'll find it."

Highly unlikely, but Paige still appreciated his optimism.

For the next thirty minutes, they retraced her steps, taking time to scour every inch of the ground between her car and the barn door and then where she'd sat playing with the goats, fol-lowed by her path for feeding each one of them.

And they came up empty.

Paige sat on the wooden bench near the door and buried her face in her filthy hands. She smelled like goat, manure and dried hay. Definitely a lovely sight.

Tears filled her eyes as her father's face appeared from her memory.

Micah sat next to her and slipped his arm around her shoulders. "I'm sorry."

She pulled off the grimy gloves and slapped them on the bench beside her. "I know it's just a stupid necklace, but it was the last gift from my dad. And it wasn't even about the necklace, but what he said when he gave it to me."

"What did he say?" Micah's rich voice, full of compassion, seeped into those cracks in her heart that hadn't quite healed in nearly fifteen years.

"My parents gave me birthday presents after dinner, then we had cake and ice cream. Funny thing is, I don't even remember what the other gifts were. But after we ate cake and ice cream, I went outside. We had this planked wooden swing suspended from our front porch ceiling. Mom had hanging plants, hummingbird feeders and wind chimes. It was such a tranquil place to sit and think. I sat on the swing, and Dad came out a few minutes later. He handed me a small black velvet box from the jewelry store. I opened it and found this delicate heart lying on a bed of satin. He put it around my neck and said, 'You stole my heart the moment we learned of your existence. When you decide to give your heart to someone, make sure it's for the right reason. Never settle.' Then, after Dad was killed, I never took it off, because it felt almost like he was there with me somehow. I'm sure that sounds silly coming from a grown woman."

"Doesn't sound silly at all." Micah pressed his cheek to the top of her head. "And you're positive you had it when you left your cottage?"

"Yes." Her voice broke as she nodded. The landscape blurred in front of her. She pulled in a deep breath and shifted her eyes to the hilltops, where bare branches scratched the sky. Swallowing several times, she struggled to maintain control of the buildup in her chest.

A tear slid down her cheek.

Followed by another. Then one more.

She turned her face into Micah's shoulder and wept for what she had lost.

Micah tightened his arm around her and pressed her against his chest. He rubbed small circles across her shoulders and upper back. And let her cry. He didn't try to fill her with empty words or promises he couldn't keep.

Feeling raw and ragged, she pulled away and rubbed the heels of her hands over her eyes and dragged her hands over her face. She blew out a strangled breath. "I'm sorry."

"Sorry for what?" His voice was so low and gentle she barely made out the words.

"For falling apart. It's only a necklace. And we have more important things to do than waste time looking for something that can be replaced."

Micah tilted her chin and captured her gaze with his. "First of all, never apologize for crying. Tears can be healing. I'm here for you. Even if you feel like you have to be strong for everyone else, I am your safe space. You don't have to stay strong for me. Second, the necklace is important to you, so it's worth taking the time to find. I'll get a flashlight and we can look through every inch of this barn if that's what it takes, then we will search the pasture."

"Micah, we have so much work to do before our next deadline. This will just have to wait."

"The longer we wait, the harder it will be to find. We'll do it now. The other work isn't going anywhere."

For the next hour, they searched the barn thoroughly, then headed for the pasture. As she moved toward the fence, Daffy and Lulu raced over to her.

"Dad has a metal detector. I'll borrow that,

then go over the barn once more. If it's there, the detector will pick it up." Micah stood behind her.

She leaned against his chest. "You've done enough. I really appreciate it. More than you know. But I have to get these chores done and head back to my cottage to shower. I have to work with a client today."

"On Saturday?"

"He was sick earlier in the week and missed his therapy session. I said I'd reschedule for today if he was better. His mom called last night."

"You are a compassionate person, Paige. I'll finish the chores, so you can head back now if you want."

"They're my goats. My responsibility. I can't allow emotions to get in the way of what needs to be done."

"Cut yourself some slack. Didn't you remind me recently that it's okay to lean on other people? We're here to help you." Micah gave her shoulder a gentle squeeze. "Ian didn't run this farm single-handedly, and he never expected you to do so as well."

Paige cupped her forehead in her hand. "I'm so tired, Micah. I wish we were done. I'm so ready to be done."

Turning her to face him, he traced a finger down the side of her cheek, slipping a stray lock of hair behind her ear. Then he caressed his knuckles over the curve of her chin, his blue eyes connecting with hers. "I know you're tired, but you are doing such a fantastic job. Just a little longer until we make our next deadline, and then we can both rest. Just think of how worth it everything will be when we're finished. As for being done, I hope you're referring to all the work and not being done with me."

She looked at him, then lowered her eyes. Without a word, she shook her head. A slight smile formed on her lips as she took his hand. "I don't think I'll ever be rid of you, will I?"

He grinned. "Not if I can help it."

Drawing her close, he lowered his head and brushed a feather-light kiss over her lips.

Her breathing hitched.

The warmth of his closeness enveloped her against the late-February chill. She rested her head against his chest and listened to his heart rhythm.

Strong and steady.

And that's how she felt when she was with him.

With him by her side, she could accomplish practically anything.

Micah kissed the top of her head, then wrapped his arm tighter around her. Then he jerked back, a scowl etching his forehead. "Um,

Paige? Just what was in that feed that you gave the goats?"

She shrugged. "I gave them the grain they eat every day. Why?"

"It appears Daffy found the Cracker Jack prize." His mouth lifted in a half grin as he pointed over her shoulder.

Paige whirled around. A silver chain hung out of the goat's mouth. She jerked out of Micah's arms and rushed through the fence, gathering the goat in her arms. "Open your mouth, you scamp."

The goat bleated, releasing a chain along with saliva into Paige's hand. Her shoulders slumped, she pocketed the chain, then wiped her hand down the side of her jeans. Still cradling Daffy, Paige turned back to Micah. "The chain was there, but the heart is missing."

Micah lifted a shoulder and held out a hand. "What goes in needs to come out eventually. We can pen her, then wait and retrieve the heart in a day or so."

Paige looked at the docile goat with her white muzzle and sweet face. Then she shook her head. "As much as I appreciate the suggestion, Micah, I don't think I could wear the necklace again knowing it was inside my goat."

Micah lifted the goat out of Paige's arms and set her inside the fenced area toward the barn.

Then he took Paige's hand. "Even though the heart is missing, the memories are still there." He tapped his own chest. "And no one can take those away from you."

As much as Paige appreciated his kind words, her heart still ached at losing the precious gift from her father.

"What your father gave you is even more special than a silver necklace. Remember that."

A wash of tears glazed her eyes as his words settled over her. She looked at the man she'd once considered a frenemy and realized she was in real danger of losing another heart—her own, despite her resolution to be cautious, to not mix business with a personal relationship.

The Micah from her childhood was gone. In his place stood a man with integrity and character. The kind of man her father had been. The kind of man she wanted in her life. And that was why she hadn't settled for second best.

She'd been waiting for Mr. Right to come along, and now he stood in front of her.

Now she had to figure out how to keep from losing him, too.

Chapter Ten

If someone had told Paige two months ago that she would've become a goat farmer and built a business from the bottom up in just a few weeks, she would've laughed.

But she wasn't laughing now.

In fact, she was feeling pretty pleased with the progress she and Micah had been making. They were still on track to meet their final deadline.

She and Micah had grown closer, losing that childish rivalry as they helped each other out.

She was going to miss not working together on a regular basis.

Sure, she'd still see him, especially with the goat farm edging against his property, but he'd be busy helping his men transition into a new way of life. And she was so proud of him for what he was doing.

But, for now, she needed to stop worrying

about what would be and focus on what still needed to be done.

She dipped the narrow roller in the paint tray and then added another coat to the wall. It was a little awkward doing it with her left hand, but she managed.

After finishing the bedrooms at Micah's house, they'd moved to the therapy barn, where the interior walls had been insulated, drywalled and primed. Now she was putting the finishing touches on the final room.

Tomorrow she could begin moving in equipment and setting up the sensory rooms.

Micah's family and hers were all pitching in to bring both places to completion, and she appreciated all they had done to pull everything together. There weren't enough words to thank everyone for what they'd done.

"Paige, there you are."

Paige turned away from the wall to find her mother standing in the doorway. "What's up?"

"I just wondered where you had disappeared to. No one's seen you since lunch. Did you even stop to eat?"

"I grabbed an apple. I wasn't really hungry for anything else. I'll eat later. Once the work is done."

"Paige, honey. Take a break. I'll finish this

wall and you go get something to eat. I think Micah is outside manning the grill."

That's what she was afraid of. If she went outside, she'd want to stay where he was, and she wouldn't get anything painted.

She smiled at her mother. "Thanks, Mom. But I'm fine. Truly. I'll finish this and then I'll grab something."

Mom gave her a look that Paige knew all too well. With her hand fisted on her hip, she looked at Paige over the rim of her glasses. Then she sighed. "Okay, fine. What can I do to help?"

Paige nodded toward the other roller. "You could do the wall by the window. Everything's taped off. The first coat needs to be added."

Her mom pulled up her sleeves, retightened her ponytail, then crossed the room and picked up the paint roller. After gliding it through the paint, she applied it to the wall. "You and Micah are spending a lot of time together."

Paige turned her attention back to the wall, adding a soft green over the primed surface. "Mom, we're partners, remember? Of course we're spending a lot of time together. We're on a deadline. And with the open house coming up, we're busier than ever."

"I know, and I understand, but things are different between you. Are you planning on continuing this…partnership after you sign the final paperwork?"

Paige dipped her roller in the tray once more. "I don't know. I mean, we haven't really talked about it. We've been so busy with everything else."

"What do you want, Paige?" Mom's calm voice tugged at Paige.

What *did* she want?

"I want to finish painting the walls, so I can mark it off my to-do list and feel an even greater sense of accomplishment. Then I want to have a successful therapy center to help children accomplish more than expected. And to be close to you and Abbs and Grandpa and Grandma."

"Those are great things, but that's not what I'm talking about. And I think you know that."

Paige wanted time to explore her growing attraction toward Micah.

Who was she kidding?

She needed to be honest with herself—it was more than an attraction.

She was falling more in love with Micah with each passing day, and that scared her more than anything.

"I want someone I can lean on, someone who will stick around when life gets tough, someone I can partner with. I want someone to make me laugh and to wipe my tears when I cry. But what if I can't have what I want, Mom?"

"What do you mean? Why do you think you can't have that?"

Paige set the roller back in the paint tray, then moved in front of the window that overlooked the backyard and the pond.

Smoke spiraled from the barbecue grill Chuck had brought down from the farm. Micah's niece and nephews, clad in colorful snow gear, tossed snowballs into the pond under their grandmother's watchful eyes. Even through the closed pane, she could hear the sound of the table saw squealing through wood as Jake, Tucker and Evan finished the work on Micah's house.

Activity all around, coming together for a common goal. Her dream was happening because of the way her family partnered with Micah's. And she couldn't be more pleased.

So why did she have this lingering heaviness in her chest?

"What if it's one or the other? What if once we sign our paperwork, Micah goes his own way? Or what if with the time it's going to take to invest in my business and Micah in his housing project, we won't be able to find time for each other?"

Her mother moved over to the window and draped an arm around Paige's shoulders. "Those are a lot of what-ifs. Focus on today, on this week, on the open house. Then, once this is behind you, you and Micah will have time to talk and work things out. Because it is possible, you know, to have both a career and a relationship. No matter what, life is always going to be busy. It's all about making choices."

Mom's words lingered as Paige retrieved the roller to finish painting the room. She was right. Instead of having an internal freak-out over imaginary what-ifs, Paige needed to focus on one thing at a time. And right now, her focus needed to be completing the task at hand.

What if Mom was right, though? What if they *could* have both? Because she was certain about one thing—she wasn't ready for their partnership to end.

Micah didn't intend to eavesdrop. He merely planned to check on Paige and see what he could do to help.

But the moment he heard his name, his footsteps paused outside the open door to one of her therapy rooms.

The smell of paint let him know Paige had beaten him to the task, even though he'd said he would take care of it so she wouldn't tax her shoulder.

Stubborn woman.

He agreed with Paige. They were partners. They did have a deadline.

But what if Mrs. Watson was right? What if it was possible for there to be more between Paige and him?

He knew how he felt. And the way she returned his kisses made him suspect Paige was feeling the same way, but he didn't know for sure. Once they signed the final paperwork, he planned to tell Paige he wanted this partnership to become a forever thing.

He was home for good.

She could trust him not to walk away.

But what if the hesitation in her voice while talking with her mother was her own struggle with admitting how she truly felt about him? Did they have a chance to be together after this was over?

He didn't have time to waste standing outside a doorway listening to mother and daughter talk about him, no matter how much he wanted to hear the rest of the conversation.

As he backed away, his cell phone went off in his back pocket. The jangly ringtone echoed through the empty space.

Heat suffused his face as he tried to silence the device. He looked up to find Paige standing in the doorway, arms crossed over her chest and a swipe of green paint on her cheek. "Sneaking up on us?"

"No, not really. I was coming to lend a hand with the painting when I heard my name."

"So you decided to listen in?"

He shrugged. "Don't tell me you wouldn't have done the same."

She lifted her chin. "I would not have stopped to listen to a private conversation."

"Oh, please, Paige." He smiled, trying to lighten the mood. "If you heard your name, you'd stop to hear what was being said about you."

Her hands moved to her hips. "I value other people's privacy. So, no, I would not, even if I had heard my name."

Micah laughed and waved away her words. "Okay, sure."

Paige huffed and turned away.

Whistling, Micah headed for the front door.

"Micah. A word?"

He turned to find Paige's mother behind him. "Hey, Mrs. W. What's up?"

"It's Wendy, remember? Go easy on my daughter. Please?"

"I'm just giving her a hard time. And to be honest, I didn't hear much of your conversation anyway. Paige just gets riled up so quickly that it's fun to egg her on."

"Maybe so, but you two aren't kids anymore. You need to learn how to communicate as adults. And the sooner the better, I say. Paige needs you, no matter how much she will deny it. And I think you need her, too." She waved her hand across the room. "I know you two are swamped with getting these programs up and going, but promise me once the open house is over, you will make time to talk with her...to really talk with her."

He didn't mind hassling Paige, especially when he could joke about his own emotions. But with the honest look on her mother's face, Micah needed to be straight with her.

He rested a hand on her arm. "I promise you, Mrs. Watson. I have every intention of having that discussion with Paige."

The worry melted off her forehead as a smile spread across her face. "Wendy."

"Yes, ma'am."

"What discussion?"

Micah looked over Wendy's shoulder to find Paige standing in the doorway, wiping her hands with a towel. He chuckled. "See? My point exactly. You heard your name and now you want to know what was being said."

"Well, of course, if it pertains to our partnership."

Wendy slipped behind him, giving his shoulders a gentle squeeze. Then she whispered, "All the best."

Paige strode across the room, her arms folded over her chest. The sunlight streaming through the window highlighted her hair, stripping it to white gold. Even dressed in her gray yoga pants, paint-spattered long-sleeved red T-shirt and sneakers, she still looked like a million bucks.

His mouth went dry.

Micah tried to swallow and ended up choking on a mouthful of air that went down the wrong way.

Gripping the door frame, Micah bent at the waist and coughed, gasping for air. Tears rushed to his eyes as his throat and chest burned.

Paige hurried over to him. "Hey, are you okay?"

He managed a nod.

She led him to a couple of folding chairs piled with paintbrushes and extension cords. She dumped them on the floor. "Have a seat. I'll go get you some water."

He sat and buried his face in his folded arm as he tried to get his breathing under control. He dug a used napkin from lunch out of his front pocket and mopped his eyes.

Paige returned with two water bottles, uncapped one and handed it to him. She sat in the chair next to him, took a drink of water, then rubbed his back. "Sure you're okay?"

If he said no, would she continue rubbing his back?

"Apparently swallowing and breathing at the same time keeps me humble…or makes me look like an idiot."

"It happens to the best of us."

"The swallowing? Or looking like an idiot?"

"Both?" She laughed, the sound settling over him like a warm, light summer rain, slipping into every pore.

She capped her bottle, then tore at the plastic wrapper. "Okay, so I was wrong. If I do hear my name in a conversation, I want to know what was being said. What were you and my mom talking about?"

Micah wrestled with his answer for a moment, debating between giving her a smart-mouth remark or speaking from his heart.

He set his water bottle on the floor between his feet, then he took her hand and rubbed his thumb across her soft skin. "Your mom wants to make sure I'm not going to hurt you."

"Are you?" She looked at him with eyes so sweet and tender that it was all he could do not to kiss her.

Releasing her hand, he touched the hair falling from her ponytail and tucked it behind her ear, trailing his finger down the side of her jaw. "It was never my intention to hurt you, Paige."

She took his hand in hers and entwined their fingers. "Good. I don't like being hurt. I've had enough for a lifetime, thank you."

"We still have a lot to do over the next couple of days before the open house on Saturday, but when it's all over, I would love for us to talk. Really talk."

"About what?" Her eyes lowered as she traced her thumb over his.

"I think you know."

"I've been wrong before, so I would really love it if you could just say it. So there's no misunderstandings in the future."

"I would love to talk about us. And the future."

She swallowed. "Do you think we have a future?"

"I do. And I believe you think so, too."

She captured his gaze and held it a moment. Then she nodded as a slow smile crept across her mouth. "I do."

Micah slid a hand around the curve of her neck. He drew her to him and brushed a kiss across her slightly parted lips, then pressed his forehead to hers. "I'm hoping the next few days go by in a blur, because I want more from you, more with you, than a few stolen moments."

"I'll take every stolen moment I can get. Especially if it means there will be more of them. And these." Her voice a little breathless, Paige reached for his hand once more and held it to her chest. Then she touched her lips to his.

For a moment, their to-do lists drifted away. For a moment, he couldn't hear the sounds of hammers, saws or directions being called between rooms. For a moment, it was all about Paige and the way he felt in her presence. But it was more than just a feeling.

He was in love with her and couldn't wait to tell her. Hopefully, she felt the same way. Otherwise, he'd end up looking like a fool.

"Hey, if you two lovebirds are about finished? The rest of us would like to get these rooms painted."

Micah and Paige jerked apart.

Evan stood in the doorway, his shoulder pressed against the doorjamb and a smirk on his face.

Grinning, Micah stood, then held out his hand to Paige, whose face matched the crimson of her shirt. "We were, uh, discussing our partnership."

Evan chuckled. "No doubt in my mind. You two make great...partners."

Still holding Paige's hand, Micah gave it a gentle squeeze and looked down at her. "Yes, we do."

No doubt in his mind.

They would make great partners. Not only in business but in life and love. Now they just had to get through the next few days so they could make time to talk about making this partnership more permanent.

Chapter Eleven

With the next deadline coming quicker than she'd like, Paige didn't have time to pull off a bridal shower, but her best friend's upcoming wedding deserved to be celebrated.

So Paige would put a smile in place and make it happen.

After all, that's what she did best.

And thankfully, her wrist and shoulder pain had subsided enough for her to handle the prep without too much hassle.

Thankfully, Natalie wanted something small and intimate, so Paige took advantage of the gorgeous winter afternoon with sun glowing across last night's fallen snow and arranged a tea on her enclosed sunporch.

She'd borrowed a large round table from church and covered it with burgundy linens, rose gold placements and a hurricane lamp sitting in a ring of eucalyptus and baby's breath. Small votives at each place setting sparkled against Betsy's china.

Last summer, Paige had hung strands of Edison lights across the ceiling. Even though the afternoon sun brightened her backyard, the lights cast a subtle glow over the table.

Expecting Willow at any minute, Paige gave the table a final glance, then returned to the kitchen. She spread homemade chicken salad on fruited walnut bread, then cut the sandwiches into triangles. Once the timer dinged, she removed the warmed ham and cheese brioche buns from the oven and set them on the cooling rack.

She sliced the small loaves of applesauce bread and arranged them around the glass dish of cranberry-swirled cream cheese. Along with scones, clotted cream and homemade jam, Paige added miniature cream puffs and raspberry lemon bars.

Her front door opened.

"Hello. Hello," Willow called from the living room.

"In the kitchen."

Willow came into the kitchen carrying two reusable grocery bags. "Hey, you should be resting. I said I'd be here to help."

Ignoring the lecture, Paige admired Willow's

teal-and-rust-colored patterned dress worn over a pair of burgundy tights and suede ankle booties. Her short tangle of curls had been tamed with a braided fabric headband. "You look cute."

"Thanks. It's fun to wear something other than scrubs for a change. I love your sweater."

Paige glanced down at the mustard-colored eyelet cardigan she wore over a navy-and-white-striped dress. "Thanks."

"How are you feeling?" Willow washed her hands at the kitchen sink.

"My wrist is better, and my shoulder's down to a dull ache at times. Meds are helping."

Her friend didn't need to know about the lack of sleep she'd been getting because it was tough to find a comfortable position.

"Okay, what do you want me to do?"

"The food's ready. I need to put water on for tea, then just wait for the ladies." She glanced at the clock. "Which should be in about fifteen minutes or so."

"Did you get a final head count?"

"There will be ten of us—Natalie, Dr. Mary, Claudia, Tori, Isabella, Olivia, my mom, my sister, you and me. My grandma couldn't make it."

Someone knocked on Paige's door.

"I guess they're a little early."

Willow waved her out of the room. "You answer the door, and I'll get the water going for tea."

Paige headed for the door, then showed the ladies to the sunporch. Within minutes, laughter filled the cottage.

Nearly three hours later, after lunch had been consumed, games had been played and gifts had been unwrapped, all with even more laughter, the party ended, leaving Paige, Willow and Natalie to talk in the solitude of the approaching evening.

Her mother had insisted on doing cleanup, and Paige had been too tired to protest.

"You guys. I can't thank you enough. Today was perfect." Natalie leaned forward, grabbed each of their hands and squeezed. "You're the best friends a girl could ask for."

Paige squeezed back, then leaned back in her chair, shaking her head. "You deserve it. I can't believe you're getting married in two weeks."

"You know, when Evan proposed on New Year's Eve, I was so ready to run off and get married the next day. But now I'm glad we waited a couple of months at least. It gave more time for Aidan to get to know his dad. Not to mention how busy we've been with managing the kennels and working on Evan's River Therapy program. But we're ready—and excited— to start our lives together." Natalie dropped her gaze to the opal engagement ring and twisted it. Then she lifted her eyes to her friends, her eyes bright. "You know, I didn't expect to be this happy."

Paige's eyes filled, but she blinked rapidly to hold them back. "Oh, Nat. You deserve it. And so much more."

Natalie brushed a manicured finger under her eyes. "Okay, enough of my sappy babble. What's going on with you two? Seems like we haven't been together in ages."

"I don't want to steal your thunder, but…" Willow reached into her pocket, slid a ring on her left hand, then held it up, revealing a sparkling diamond. "Last night, Julian asked me to marry him. I would have called you both then, but I really wanted to tell you in person."

Natalie and Paige squealed, rushed out of their chairs and hugged their friend.

"I'm so happy for you." Paige hugged Willow once again.

And she was.

Both of her friends, with their difficult childhoods, deserved to have someone to love and cherish them. But she still couldn't stop that little niggle inside her that clamored, when would it be her turn?

She didn't need to tie her happiness to a man.

After all, she was an educated woman who was about to launch her own therapy practice.

But still…

It would be nice to have that loving support her friends found with their fiancés.

"You okay, Paige? You got quiet all of a sudden."

Paige pasted a bright smile in place. "Yes, of course. I was just thinking about how much you two deserve to be this happy. I'm so excited for both of you."

"What about you?" Natalie and Willow exchanged looks.

"What about me?"

Nat twisted her engagement ring. "How are things going with you and Micah?"

"Micah? We're just friends. Partners. That's it." Paige lifted a shoulder, then reached for her nearly empty teacup.

"Friends who kiss, apparently." Willow raised an eyebrow.

"I may regret telling you about those."

"Those? There's been more than one?"

Paige lowered her eyes as she lifted her cup. "Maybe."

Willow traced her finger over her sparkling ring. "It begins with a kiss."

"I don't know. It's different with Micah. Sometimes I'm not sure he even likes me, let alone feels anything deeper." But he did mention wanting to talk about their future, so that had to count for something. Right?

Nat and Will exchanged glances, then grinned. "He likes you."

"We have so much going on right now. There's no time for anything else."

"Do you like him?" Nat stood and moved behind Paige, bracing her hands on the back of the chair.

Paige looked up at her. "What? Of course."

"No, do you *like* him?"

"What is this? Third grade?"

Nat squeezed her shoulder. "I'm guessing yes. Otherwise your face wouldn't be getting so red."

"You two are impossible." Shaking her head, Paige stood and moved to the window facing the backyard, arms wrapped around her waist.

Willow stood next to her and nudged her shoulder. "If you like him, step out of your comfort zone and see if there is potential for the two of you."

"What if I do and he doesn't want me?"

"He wants you." Nat moved to the other side of her.

"How do you know?"

"We've seen the way he looks at you, and it's not just as friends. That boy is hooked." Nat looked at her. "Question is—what are you going to do about it?"

Paige didn't have an answer.

Micah just wanted to fit in with his brothers today.

And for that to happen, he needed to get over himself. Beginning with having to redo his half Windsor knot for the third time and finish getting fitted for the tux he was going to wear in his brother's wedding in less than two weeks.

After Jake had taken a rare day off from the farm, the five Holland men had headed into Shelby Lake to Emily's Bridal for their final fittings to appease a stressed Natalie. Then they planned to chow down on some wings and do some ax throwing with Evan's former kayaking teammates for his brother's bachelor party.

Micah adjusted the tails of the tie he'd finally managed to get even.

"Looking sharp, brother." Tuck moved behind him and settled his hands on Micah's shoulders. "Love the tailoring on the jacket."

"Me, too. Now I won't have an empty sleeve hanging loose." He touched the jacket shoulder where the sleeve had been removed and the arm opening stitched shut. "Who knew there was adaptive menswear?"

Evan ruffled Micah's hair as he walked past,

strutting in his identical tux except with a rose gold vest and tie. "Are you planning on getting this mop chopped?"

Micah batted away his brother's hand and smoothed down his hair. "Do you really think I love you that much?"

"Oh, so if you really loved me, then you'd get it cut?" He lifted his arms and shrugged. "Hey, I told Nat I'd ask."

"Since when does Nat care about my hair? Besides, your wedding's not for another couple of weeks. Who knows what will happen between now and then?"

"Especially with Paige." Tuck winked at him as he joined them in front of the mirror and straightened his own tie.

"Paige and I are friends. Business partners."

Turning away from the mirror, Evan shrugged out of his jacket and removed his vest. "Seriously, though, I saw what I interrupted the other day. Paige isn't the type to kiss just anyone. You two have the beginning of something special going on."

Micah shoved his hand in his pocket. "We're getting along really well. Our programs are coming together. And for the first time in a long time, I can look to the future."

Evan grinned. "So glad to hear it."

"And don't be blabbing to your fiancée about

what I said, either. I don't need her trying to play matchmaker."

Evan's face twisted in mock innocence as he jerked his thumbs toward his chest. "Who, me? I won't say a word. Let's get out of these penguin suits. I'm ready to scarf down some wings."

Micah swallowed a sigh. When he'd learned about the events of the day, he'd known it was going to be a challenge keeping up with his able-bodied brothers. But the last thing he wanted was for them to think that he wasn't able to pull his own. And he did love eating dripping buffalo wings. Doing it one-handed without making a mess was going to be a challenge, though.

But this was Evan's day, and Micah wasn't going to be a downer.

Back in their street clothes, Micah, Evan, Tuck, Jake and their dad piled into Jake's extended cab truck. Dad rode shotgun, leaving Evan, Tuck and Micah shoulder to shoulder in the back seat.

Twenty minutes later, Jake crossed the border into New York and parked in front of The Bullseye, a sports restaurant that advertised all-you-can-eat buckets of wings and ax-throwing pits in the basement. The guys climbed out of the truck and headed inside.

Micah's mouth watered as soon as he smelled

the tantalizing scents of grilled meat and tangy sauce.

Multiple widescreen TVs showing different sporting events hung from gleaming wooden beams around the perimeter of the dining room.

After getting settled at their table and placing their wing orders, Dad cleared his throat and picked up his glass of iced tea. "It's not often a father gets to have time together with all his boys now that they're grown and living their own lives. I'm mighty grateful. And so proud of each one of you and all that you're accomplishing."

Micah rubbed a fist against the tightness in his chest. When was the last time he'd made his father proud?

They raised their glasses, his brothers' eyes suspiciously bright, too.

Micah turned toward Evan and lifted his glass once again. "And here's to you, brother. Last summer was tough, but you powered through. Even though your career has changed, you gained a son and you're about to marry a pretty cool chick. What she sees in you, I'll never understand, but here's to Evan and Natalie. May this just be the beginning of your amazing life together."

Evan tapped his glass against Micah's. "Thanks,

man. Who knows—pretty soon, we may be celebrating with you."

Micah set his glass down and grabbed a handful of complimentary popcorn from the middle of the table.

Dad leaned forward and tapped the table in front of Micah. "Oh, hey. Claudia wanted me to mention she finished designing the gardens around the pond. She went through some of the old pictures Betsy had taken, and she got it as close as possible."

"Thanks, I'll drop by the farmhouse tomorrow and see what she's come up with. I'm not a gardener, so I'm glad she volunteered to make the pond nice again once the snow melts. She found some stained-glass water lilies that look pretty cool, so we're going to see how well they do. I want to replace the current footbridge with one that's wide enough for wheelchair access."

"I can give you a hand with that, if you'd like. Planning to restock the pond?"

Micah shot a look at Jake, who listened to the conversation but didn't add anything. In fact, Jake and Micah had spoken very little since their last blowup. "Yeah, I think so. Fishing is therapeutic. I'm sure the guys would love it."

Their server arrived with their buckets of wings and baskets of celery with blue cheese, putting an end to the conversations.

Dad prayed, then they dug in. Now that the spotlight was off him, Micah could eat his wings without feeling like he was on display.

After chowing through a few buckets of wings and then griping about the pain in their guts, they left the table and headed downstairs to where the basement had been remodeled into an ax-throwing pit.

Eight lanes constructed of two-by-fours and protective wire fencing ran parallel to one another. A plywood bull's-eye pocked with hatchet marks had been centered on the wall in each lane. A chalkboard for names and scores hung on the wall back by the throwing tables.

An ax master named Jaxon greeted them, showed them to their lane, then went over the rules. He showed them how to chalk their hands, line up their throws, then demonstrated a two-handed throw. Seeing Micah, he then demonstrated a one-handed throw, the hatchet hitting the center with a solid thwack.

While they waited for Evan's buddies to arrive, Jake and Tuck took turns throwing for fun without keeping score.

Micah leaned his elbow against one of the high-top tables behind their throwing lane. Evan slapped him on the back. "You know, man, once all this wedding stuff is over and Nat and I are back from our honeymoon, I'd really love to sit down with you to show how I could include your men in my adaptive watersports program."

"Include them how?"

"Include them in the training of using the kayaks. Then they could help me throughout the season. Plus, I want to create a series of videos to help other people with physical disabilities to have safe yet fun adventures on the water. You think they'd be up for that?"

Micah shrugged. "Sure, it wouldn't hurt to ask. What about the guys in the Fatigues to Farming program?"

"They don't mind blowing off steam, but they're more focused on learning the farming aspect. Do you know how you want to tie your program in with Fatigues to Farming?"

"Not quite. After my blowup with Jake at the farmhouse, I kind of put it out of my mind. I'm modeling the transitional house similar to Phil's, but I don't even know how many guys are coming yet. Even though Shelby Lake doesn't have a homeless population like the cities, Phil and I will work together to offer housing for the men he ministers—if they want to come, that is."

Evan gave Micah's shoulder a gentle squeeze. "Well, say the word, and I'd love to help in any way I can. I'm proud of what you're doing. And it's great to have you back home again."

Home. There was that word again, and more

and more, he wanted to accept it, lean into it. With Paige. With his family.

It'd been so long since he'd claimed Shelby Lake as home, but maybe it was possible, after all, to put the past to rest and focus on his future. Growing up, Evan had always had Micah's back. And now, his brother's support meant more than Micah could say.

Tuck's phone went off. He pulled it out of his back pocket and answered. His eyes shot to Micah, then he turned slightly and spoke into his phone. He ended his call, set his hatchet on the holding table and snatched his coat off the hook behind the lane. "We gotta go."

"What's going on, Tuck?" Dad reached for his leather jacket.

Tuck locked eyes with Micah. "Structure fire on Holland Hill. The goat barn's on fire."

Micah felt the color drain from his face as a chill slithered down his back. "Paige. Is she okay?"

"She's safe, but the barn's engulfed. It's not good."

Back in Jake's truck, Micah cupped a hand over his eyes and whispered the only thing that came to mind. "Why, God? Why?"

Chapter Twelve

Today was supposed to be a day of fun. To celebrate her best friend's upcoming wedding.

And now it was marred by tragedy.

Paige wanted to scream. To cry. To shake her fist and rail against the injustice of it all.

But she couldn't.

Every time she tried to open her mouth, not a sound escaped.

Nothing to voice the horror unfolding before her.

All she could do was stare at the flames licking the sides of the goat barn and prowling across the roof, stalking and ready to devour anything in their heated path.

Rotating red and blue emergency lights reflected off the coal-black sky, highlighting the skeletal remains of her dream vanishing before her.

Firefighters in turnout gear snaked hoses across the snow as they battled the beast, the heat melting the snow around the barn.

Acrid black smoke puffed and snaked from the structure, burning her eyes and choking her throat. Flying ash spiraled through the air and landed in the snow, only to be extinguished.

Like her future.

In the distance, goats that had managed to escape before the blaze consumed their home bleated from the pasture. Their anguished cries shredded her heart.

And there was nothing she could do to help them.

If it weren't for Grandpa's strong arms holding on to her, preventing her from rushing into the belly of the blaze, she would've collapsed in the snowy field where they stood, numb and watching.

For the hundredth time since she'd gotten the call about smoke coming from the barn and raced down the road to find the wooden structure engulfed, she went through every step of her last visit.

After Natalie's bridal shower, Paige had headed to the barn to feed and water the goats. She'd turned on the heat lamps to add a little warmth while she was there. After checking on Buttons and her kids, she'd made sure all the heat lamps had been unplugged and put away. She was sure of it. She remembered unplugging the heat lamp…right?

She'd unplugged it.

Didn't she?

A fresh wave of grief washed over her as the events from earlier in the evening muddled in her head.

"Paige!"

At the sound of her name, she turned in Grandpa's arms to find Micah racing out of his brother's truck and coming toward her.

She pulled free and hurried toward him.

Micah caught her in his grip so tightly her feet lifted off the ground. He buried his face in her hair. "Oh, thank God, you're safe."

Paige wrapped her arms around his neck and curled her fingers around the back of his shirt. She buried her face against his chest, and for the first time, she released the pain that nearly gutted her. He held her as she sobbed, his fingers cupping the back of her head, holding her close in his strong, protective grip.

He murmured quiet, soothing words into her hair, but she couldn't make them out with all the noise around them.

Needing a breath, she pulled back and ground the heels of her mittened hands into her eyes. She looked up at him. "I can't remember if I unplugged the heat lamp. What if this is my fault? What if I caused this?"

He folded her into the cradle of his chest once again. "Paige, whatever caused the fire was an accident. Don't beat yourself up about it." His words vibrated from the rumble in his chest against her ear.

She wanted to believe him. But she just couldn't remember about the heat lamp.

Tucker trudged across the road and settled a hand on her shoulder. "I'm sorry, Paige."

She could only nod, her cheek resting against the softness of Micah's flannel shirt as he tightened his hold.

"What do you know, Tuck?"

"I just talked with the chief. Apparently, a passerby saw the smoke and called 911. Then the guy stopped at the farmhouse and told Claudia. She called Paige's grandparents, then called me. They feel the house and pole barn will be safe, but they're hosing them down should any stray sparks get loose. The barn is a total loss."

"And the goats?" Her voice caught.

"There's no way to know how many escaped before the fire consumed the structure. I'm really sorry." Tucker gave her shoulder a gentle squeeze.

Another surge of tears washed over Paige's gritty eyes. "What am I going to, Micah? The open house is in a week, and without goats, it's tough to have an animal-assisted practice."

He tipped up her chin. "I don't know, but whatever it is, you won't have to do it alone. Let's get through the night and see what morning brings."

She didn't have to wait. She knew.

Morning would bring the death of her dream. And it was all her fault.

If only she could remember about the lamp.

Paige didn't want to leave the security of her bed. But somehow she had to figure out how to be an adult today despite no sleep and the terror replaying over and over in her head.

Even after an extra-long shower to thaw her from the inside out and to wash away the stench of the smoke seared into her skin, Paige couldn't get warm.

Every time she closed her eyes, all she could see was the barn engulfed in flames. And hear the panicked bleating of the goats in the pasture.

Last night—or early this morning—she'd refused to leave until the firefighters claimed victory over the blaze and headed back to their stations.

Now she needed to move and see how many goats had survived. And do what she could to salvage her business.

With a sigh that gripped her ribs as it slid out of her chest, Paige threw back her comforter and climbed out of bed. After dressing in jeans, a soft sweatshirt and thick socks, she made her way to the kitchen to make a cup of tea.

A knock sounded on her door.

Changing paths, she headed through the living room and opened the door. Micah stood on the porch holding a cup carrier and a paper bag. "Good morning. I brought you some breakfast."

"Thanks." She stepped back to allow him to enter. She appreciated the gesture and didn't have the heart to tell him she had no appetite.

He looked around the room. "Where's Charlotte? Usually she barks when I knock."

Paige nodded toward her grandparents' house. "She's with my grandma. She and Abby took care of her last night while I was at the fire. I'll bring her home later."

Micah carried the cups and food to the kitchen and set them on her small table. Then he turned and held out his arm.

Without a word, she walked into his embrace, breathing in the clean scent from his pullover as she pressed her cheek to his chest. His arm tightened around her.

Paige closed her eyes against a fresh rush of tears and forced back the knot jammed in her throat. "I need to head to the barn and check on the goats. I have to arrange for cleanup, talk with the contractor about rebuilding the barn and—" She stopped speaking as the weight of what needed to be done pressed on her shoulders.

Micah released her and guided her to one of the chairs. Then he opened the plastic top of the to-go cup and handed it to her. He opened the bag, pulled out a recyclable to-go box and popped the lid with his thumb. "Drink some tea. I stopped at Joe's and Isabella whipped up a couple of breakfast sandwiches. Eat that, then you're coming with me."

She eyed the English muffin sandwich with egg, cheese and ham, and shook her head, pushing it away. "Thanks, but I'm not hungry right now."

He pushed it back toward her. "You need to eat."

"Fine." She took a small bite, then set the sandwich back in the box. Any other time she loved Isabella's cooking, but today the food slid down her throat like wet cement.

"Paige, do you trust me?"

She looked at him, her eyes searching his face. He had to be as tired as she was, especially after insisting on driving her home and making sure she was safely inside before he left. She nodded and cupped his cheek. "Yes, I trust you."

The four words unshackled some of the doubts that had been pinned to her heart for so long. But over the weeks they'd been working together, Micah had done nothing but stay true to his word. "Why?"

He gathered their unfinished breakfast sandwiches, stuffed them in the bag, then put her tea and his coffee back in the beverage carrier. "I want you to come with me."

"Where are we going?"

"Just trust me."

Realizing she had to make a choice to take him at his word or stay in her cottage and wallow in the misery from last night's events, Paige headed for the bathroom. She washed her face, brushed her teeth and pulled her hair back into a ponytail.

Then she found her parka and started to slide her arm into the sleeve when the stench of the fire coated the back of her throat. Making a face, she pulled it off and dropped it on her bedroom floor to be washed later. She found a fleece-lined jacket and put it on, then let Micah lead her out the door and to his SUV.

As they drove the short distance from her cottage to the goat farm, they passed cars and trucks lining both sides of the road. "What's going on?"

"You'll see." He parked in the driveway in

front of the house, then came around to open her door.

She stepped out and faced the blackened ground where the barn used to stand. Her eyes widened at the number of people gathered in the barnyard.

Micah took her hand and led her across the yard. Grandpa and Chuck Holland spoke to the group, but she and Micah were too far away to hear what was being said.

She stopped and tugged gently on Micah's hand. "What's going on?" she repeated.

He released her and waved across the land. "These are your family and friends, Paige. And we want to help. To show you're not alone."

She pressed a hand to her mouth and shook her head. "I don't know what to say."

"Just say thank you."

She looked at him. "You organized this?"

"With some help from Dad and your grandfather. I called Ginny, who contacted the insurance company. They've already sent out an adjuster to review the damages. Dad notified the local authorities to be sure there's no contaminated water runoff. Jake, Tuck and Evan have been walking the pasture, rounding up goats. They're moving them to one of our barns until we can get yours rebuilt."

"Why would they do this?"

"Why not? Because neighbors help neighbors. They care about you."

Cupping her forehead against the ray of sunshine edging through the bare trees above the pole barn, Paige couldn't quite articulate the sense of peace that washed over her. No, she didn't have to handle everything on her own. She scoured the pasture to see if any of the goats were in view. "Do you know how many goats were spared?"

"Not yet. We'll have a full head count once my brothers get them rounded up."

She nodded and tried not to think the worst. She lifted her arms, then dropped them back at her side. "I don't know what I should be doing."

"How about if I take you back home so you can get some rest?"

She eyed the skeletal remains of the barn, then turned her back to it. "This is my mess. I should be cleaning it up."

"By yourself? Why not trust it to the people who know what they're doing?"

He was right. And she knew that. It just didn't sit well with her. Her shoulders sagged. She felt if she closed her eyes, she'd fall asleep on her feet.

The wind picked up, whisking her cheeks. She buried her hands in her coat pockets and looked at Micah. "Okay, fine. I'll go back home and get some sleep. Then I'm going to dig in and help, no matter what needs to be done."

He looped his arm around her shoulders and pulled her against him, dropping a kiss on her chilled forehead. "That's my girl."

Oh, the idea of her being his girl…

He guided her back to his SUV and opened the passenger side door. "Once you get some rest, I'll come back and get you. Then I'll do whatever you ask of me to help."

"Even dress up in a goat costume for the open house?"

"If that's what it would take to get the smile to return to your beautiful face, then consider it done."

Her lips twitched. "I'd pay good money to see that."

He dropped a kiss on the top of her head and tucked her back in the passenger seat.

What if she asked him not to break her heart? Would he be able to promise that? Because she was at the point of no return when it came to how she felt about Micah.

Chapter Thirteen

Paige couldn't believe what had been accomplished in less than a week.

With neighbors and crews pitching in from sunup to sundown, the barn remains had been leveled and all the debris had been hauled away, leaving nothing but a dark patch of earth to show that something had been there. Micah's house had been used to prepare meals and to offer warmth and respite for the workers who put in long hours.

She needed to make a whole lot of cookies as a way of saying thanks.

Paige and Micah had spent several hours talking with a contractor working with the insurance company about rebuilding. The contractor had assumed they were a couple, and neither one had corrected him.

Despite all the good that had happened,

Paige's heart ached for the loss of the goats she'd come to love—about half her herd had perished in the fire, including Buttons and her kids, whom Paige hadn't even named yet.

Rosie, Daffy and Lulu, her ultimate escape artists, had survived and hung out with the others in one of the Holland barns. She tried to visit as often as she could, which was tough as they did the final cleaning and setup at Micah's house and in her therapy barn.

She continued to thank God both of those buildings had been spared.

And somehow Micah and Tori had managed to get her to agree to continue with the open house as planned, even though she wasn't sure about the state of her business yet.

After all, it was for Micah's program, too.

So she managed to keep her smile firmly in place as she wove through the crowd answering questions, accepting condolences about the fire and hugging friends.

At least the preliminary reports proved she hadn't been to blame. Instead, an electrical short caused the blaze. It may have lifted one burden, but her heart still ached at the losses.

And after talking with Ginny, the fire didn't create a setback in meeting their goals as Paige had feared. She and Micah would meet with her in a week and sign the final paperwork.

All the hard work had been worth it.

And truth be told, she'd probably come out a better person on the other side.

Even though she and Micah wanted to keep the open house small, fifty people or so roamed through the therapy barn and Micah's house, listening to their plans for each of the programs.

Despite the chill pinching faces, no one seemed to mind the crisp temperatures. The sun cast a brilliant glow over the field on the other side of the road, where people dressed in flannels, warm jackets, hats and mittens waited to be taken on a sleigh ride pulled by the Hollands' two quarter horses, Westley and Buttercup.

Phil and his men from the Next Step had driven up from Pittsburgh, surprising Micah, to celebrate the open house with them. She had seen Micah embracing them earlier, but then she lost track of him in the crowd.

Where had he disappeared to? Hopefully he wouldn't feel overwhelmed by so many people.

Someone tapped her on the shoulder, and she turned, nearly jumping out of her skin when her face met a furry chest.

Shading her eyes, she took a step back, then let out a laugh. "You did it. You actually did it."

"Meh." Micah bleated and crunched on a nubby carrot with the leafy greens still attached. He wore a brown furry billy goat costume, complete with horns and a snowy beard. "I said I'd do it if it would bring your smile back. Does this mean I'm the best goat ever? You know—the greatest of all time?"

"You've goat to be kidding me, right?"

Micah wrinkled his face. "Okay, maybe we need to go easy on the puns for a while. It would be baaad to use them up all at once."

Paige laughed again and nudged his shoulder with hers. "The turnout has been great. I'm so pleased."

"Me, too. You hungry?" He pointed his carrot toward her. "Want a bite of my carrot?"

"No, thanks. I make it a practice not to share food with goats."

"Not even the greatest goat of all time?"

"No, you go ahead. I wouldn't want to deprive you of such a delectable treat. I'll go find something in a bit."

Still holding his carrot, Micah shaded his eyes and looked to the sky. "Ian would be thrilled to see his kites being flown. Thanks for suggesting we bring them out."

"Flying them in Ian's memory enables his legacy to continue." Tears clouded her vision as she shaded her eyes to see the multicolored kites dotting the brilliant blue sky.

Today was not about being sad.

"Ian's legacy will continue through the gifts

he has given us. Because of his generosity, we will be able to help others in ways that allow them to succeed." Micah dropped his arm over her shoulder and pressed his cheek to the top of her head.

She snuggled closer, not caring that they were in public view and she was hugging a man-size goat. She had a feeling after today things were going to be different between the two of them anyway.

She planned to talk with Micah after the open house. To tell him how she felt and to see where she stood with him. She didn't want to rush the afternoon away, but she was looking forward to having alone time with him.

Dressed in a pink parka with a gray scarf wrapped around her throat, Tori strode toward them. "Hey, guys. There's a reporter from the paper and one from the news station who would like to talk with you. Are you willing to do an interview?"

Paige's stomach tightened. She hadn't expected to give interviews, but she had spent the past couple of hours talking to family and friends about their programs, so this wouldn't be much different. Right?

Besides, the extra coverage would be good for their businesses. The quicker she got her practice going, the faster she could help more children.

They headed back inside the therapy barn, where Micah and Paige found a couple of empty chairs in the newly decorated reception area and carried them to a quiet corner.

Paige shed her long coat, revealing the same royal blue dress she'd worn to Ian's funeral, hoping the happiness of the day would erase the sad memories. For the next ten minutes, the reporter asked them questions, expressing sympathies about Paige's loss and ribbing Micah about wearing the goat costume.

A small crowd had formed behind the crew to watch, which did little to ease Paige's anxieties, but she tried to tune them out and focus on the questions the reporter asked.

After Micah finished sharing his vision for A Hand Up, the reporter asked, "Did your previous arrest impact your decision to open a transitional home for men who need a hand up?"

Wait. What?

Paige froze as her eyes darted between Micah and the reporter. Micah would've told her he'd been arrested. Wouldn't he?

His face had turned to stone.

A chill stroked her spine. She closed her eyes a second and pulled in a breath. Exhaling slowly, she looked at Micah and placed a hand on his arm, lowering her voice. "Micah? When were you arrested?"

His eyes hardened as his jaw clenched. Gently, he shook her hand off, and slowly, he rose to his feet. He swallowed, shot a look at Paige that she couldn't quite decipher, then he gave the reporter a stiff nod. "Yes, it had everything to do with it. I believe people deserve a second chance, and I want to help give it to them."

Without another word, Micah turned and pushed through the gathered crowd.

She pasted a smile in place as the reporter directed another question at her. She murmured a reply, but her focus stayed on Micah's retreating back.

She wanted nothing more than to go after her *partner* and demand why he hadn't shared his arrest with her.

Apparently, trust was one-sided for him, because he certainly didn't trust her enough to confide in her.

She answered a couple more questions, bringing the interview to an end. Tori stepped in and announced that drawings for prizes donated by community businesses would happen in about five minutes.

Paige excused herself and ran outside, searching the property for Micah. But she couldn't find him.

How hard was it to lose a grown man in a goat costume?

He shouldn't have left.

But after the reporter blindsided him with that question, he couldn't even look at Paige. Couldn't see the shock in her eyes. Or the pity.

Even as he wove his way through the crowd, the whispers trailed after him, taunting him for his failure.

He was only as good as his mistakes.

No doubt by tomorrow his program would be toast. And he had only himself to blame.

But now he had to face his family and tell them what he'd been holding back for the last year. As Micah tried to wrangle himself out of the stupid goat costume, his dad texted, asking him to come to the farmhouse.

He was twelve years old all over again and needed to face the consequences of his actions.

He trudged up the steps to the back deck, opened the door that led into the kitchen and stepped inside. Apparently, he was the last one to join the party.

His father and his brothers stood in the kitchen with coffee cups in their hands. And their expressions told him just how they really felt.

Dad gave him a grim smile. "Micah."

Shoving his hand in his front pocket, Micah nodded to his father. "Dad."

Glaring, Jake cupped his coffee mug and slammed it on the counter. "Micah, what were you thinking? Why didn't you tell us you'd been arrested? Do you realize how irresponsible it was not to share so we could get ahead of this?"

Micah lifted a shoulder. "Frankly, because it wasn't any of your business, big brother."

Jake drew a wide ring about the guys with his finger and took a step toward Micah. "Sure, it is. Especially when it affects us."

"Just how does it affect you?"

Tucker pressed a hand on Jake's shoulder. He backed off and slumped against the sink and folded his arms over his chest. Tuck pulled a cup out of the cabinet, filled it with coffee and handed it to Micah. "Is this why you couldn't make it to my wedding?"

Despite his brother's neutral tone, Micah could hear the hurt tethered to his words. He dropped his gaze to his feet and nodded.

"Son, I get why you might not have wanted to share with your brothers, but why didn't you tell me?"

"You?" Micah's head jerked up as he waved his hand over the room. "For this reason right here. I didn't want to disappoint you. I didn't want to let you down."

Jake scoffed.

Micah set his coffee on the table, curled his hand into a fist and moved in front of his brother, standing nose to nose. "You've had a problem with me since you came home from the Corps after Mom was killed and blamed me for her death. So if you have something else to say, spit it out right now."

Jake's nostrils flared as his eyes flashed. "You've always been reckless and irresponsible. You think of no one else but yourself."

"I'm sorry, Jake, that we can't all be perfect like you. Oh wait, why did you enlist in the Marine Corps again? That's right—you lost your precious college scholarship for underage drinking. So I guess your halo isn't as polished as you want everyone to think."

"I've made up for my past mistakes."

"So. Have. I."

"Oh really? How do you expect to run a transitional home for veterans with issues when you haven't even come to terms with your own?"

"You're a real jerk, you know that? I've spent the last year owning up for what I've done and redeeming myself from past mistakes. But apparently that's not good enough for you. You're the only one who can't see it because you're blinded by your own lack of faith in me."

Dad cut between them and pressed a firm hand on each of their chests. "All right, knock it off right now. Both of you." He pushed Micah away from Jake. "Take a step back and simmer down. Tell us what happened."

Micah dragged a hand over his face, the adrenaline still sluicing through his veins. "When I worked at the homeless shelter, I got to talking with a few of the guys who came in on a regular basis for meals and a bed. Apparently, I thought I could be some sort of a mentor or something, I guess. Bob, the director of the shelter, had said I had a way with earning their trust. One of the guys got some upsetting news and went on a bender. He stopped coming into the shelter. No one had seen him around. After walking the streets looking for him, I found him in a bar. I tried to get him to leave, only to learn he was hustling a couple of pool players. A brawl broke out when one of the jerks made nasty comments about my missing arm and tried to take a swing at me. I clocked him, breaking his nose. I ended up getting arrested and spent the night in jail."

"And that's when you called Ian and not me." It wasn't a question, but a statement. The hurt in his father's eyes was like a punch to Micah's gut.

"Ian bailed me out of jail, listened to my side of the story, then put me in touch with Phil. The guy I punched tried to file charges, but there were enough witnesses to prove it was self-defense. For the past six months, I've been seeing a counselor and working with Phil to help these guys get off the streets and regain some semblance of hope for their lives. I know I screwed up, but I made a promise to Ian and Phil that I'd stay out of trouble, and I kept my word."

Dad scrubbed a hand over the back of his neck. "That's admirable, Micah. But you still could have told us. We are Holland Strong, remember? With what this family's gone through over the past eight years, we could've helped you, too."

"No, Dad, I couldn't have. Jake's always going to think the worst of me. He sees a photo or hears a question and jumps to conclusions."

"Maybe it's because you're too busy buggin' out on the family to stop and explain," Jake said.

"I'm your brother, Jake. You should have my back, no matter what. To you, I will always be Micah the Menace."

"If the behavior fits…"

Jake's words ignited a fire in Micah's chest. Before he could think, he curled his fingers into a fist, pulled back his arm and let it fly toward Jake.

Except Dad chose that moment to step back between them.

Micah's fist connected with his father's jaw, the crack echoing in the kitchen as his dad's head flung sideways and smacked against the stove. He crumpled to the floor.

Micah's eyes grew wide as the horror of his actions ignited a burning in his chest. A cold sweat slicked Micah's skin.

What had he done?

He drew in a strangled breath and stretched out his hand to his father. "Dad..."

"You've done enough. Get out of here." Jake shoved him toward the door, the words ground out between clenched teeth.

Micah stumbled backward, his eyes volleying between his brothers. Tucker snatched a bag of frozen vegetables out of the freezer, then pressed it gently against their father's face.

Evan, the one who'd always been quick to jump to Micah's defense when they were kids, glared at him as he turned to wet a dishrag in the sink. Turning his back to Micah, Evan crouched in front of Dad and handed him the cloth.

Standing on the fringes once again, Micah had no one to blame but himself.

With his eyes still on his family, Micah backed up until his shoulders pushed against the back door. He rushed outside, down the steps and across to the barnyard where he'd parked his SUV.

Jake was right.

He was reckless. And irresponsible.

Once Micah the Menace, always Micah the Menace.

He rammed himself behind the wheel of his SUV and gunned the engine. He backed out, gravel spitting beneath his tires. Then he turned and headed down the hill, putting the farm in his rearview mirror.

More than anything, Micah wanted to keep driving. But he turned into Ian's driveway and jerked to a stop.

Paige sat on his front step, her coat pulled tight around her. Seeing him, she stood and waited.

Perfect. Absolutely perfect.

One more person to witness his failure.

Turning off the vehicle, he slammed the door behind him and strode past her and into the house without saying a word.

"Where have you been?" She followed him inside. "Micah, we need to talk."

He whirled around, his chest heaving. "What more is there to say?"

She put up her hands in a calm-down gesture and spoke softly. "What was that reporter talking about? When were you arrested?"

"Forget it, Paige. It doesn't matter."

"It matters to me. It matters to the future of this home. It matters to my business. But instead of talking, you ran out on me, leaving me to carry the rest of the open house by myself."

"Is that what this is about? Your business? If that's the case, then no worries. I'll be out of your hair very shortly, then your business will be safe and sound."

"What are you talking about?"

Instead of answering, he threw open the attic door and took the stairs two at a time. He grabbed his duffel out of the antique wardrobe his stepmother had refinished and opened one of the drawers, grabbing a handful of folded T-shirts.

"So you're leaving? Just like that? No discussion?"

He turned to find her standing at the top of the steps, her arms folded over her chest and her eyes shimmering with a wash of tears.

His chin dropped to his chest as he released the duffel bag on his bed. "What do you want from me, Paige?"

"I want you to talk to me. What happened? You know you can tell me anything. I just need to know what's going on. Is there anything else I should know?"

"Are you implying I'm keeping secrets from

you? I have been nothing but honest with you from the moment I saw you in the driveway when all this started. You were the one person I had hoped would be on my side, but instead of believing in me, you want to know what else I'm keeping from you." Slowly, he shook his head as he dragged his hand over his face. "The truth is I'm a screwup. That's all I will ever be. Without my family having my back and Ian gone, this…" He waved his arm over the house. "This will never work."

She hurried across the room and grabbed his arm. "No, Micah. That's not true. I'm not implying anything. I just want to know what's going on. What about us? What about our partnership? Are you leaving?"

He closed up his duffel and threw it over his shoulder. Then he touched her cheek, imprinting the petal softness of her skin one last time in his memory. "Don't you see? There won't be an us. No matter how hard I try, I will never be good enough. For my family. For you. I don't belong here. I never did, and it's time to stop fooling myself into thinking I could."

Without another word, he pushed past her and headed down the steps and out the door, leaving his future behind him.

Chapter Fourteen

How could Micah say there was no *us*?

If he thought she was going to stand there and watch him destroy what they were building, then he had another thing coming. He wasn't going to throw away their hard work for the past couple of months because of one reporter's question.

He might be ready to give up, but she wasn't. She hurried off the porch and raced down the driveway, waving her arms to get his attention as he backed out. "Micah!"

He braked and waited.

She ran over to the driver's side window and pounded on it.

Micah lowered the window, his face drawn and shoulders slumped as he gripped the steering wheel. "What do you want, Paige?"

Chest heaving and heart racing, she cupped his jaw, forcing him to look at her. Her words slid out between clenched teeth. "I want you to keep your promise. You said I could trust you, I could rely on you, that you have changed, that you weren't going anywhere. And I finally believed you. But instead of fighting for what's right, fighting for us, you're running away. If you leave right now, then your word is meaningless."

"What about your word, Paige? Huh?"

"What are you talking about?"

"You say you want someone to lean on, but you struggle to accept any help that's being offered. You always have to do things your way. If you don't let me in, then how can we have any sort of relationship?"

"I changed. You saw it. I accepted help when so many rushed to rebuild after the fire. But you're a good one to talk about letting anyone in. You grow your hair long and wear a beard to cover your scars. You're so afraid of what other people will think and hide behind your disability instead of allowing anyone to see who you really are."

"Whatever, Paige." He shifted the engine. "I gotta go."

She gripped the door frame as she wrestled with the words on her tongue. Her chest tightened as her eyes filled. She swallowed several times to move the lump growing in her throat.

She closed her eyes against the mounting pressure, but a single tear slid down her cheek. "Don't go. Please stay. For me."

Resting an elbow on the steering wheel, Micah covered his eyes. "Please don't cry, Paige. I can't handle that on top of everything else. I need some space. Time to clear my head."

Biting her lower lip, she took a step back and dashed the wetness off her face. "Space. From me."

"From you. From the house. From my family."

She looked off into the distance, the landscape blurring like watercolors. Then she turned back to face him. She gave him a slight nod and shoved her hands in her coat pockets. "Fine. I'll give you space. Take all the time you need. Just don't expect me to be here when you get back." Without another word, she turned on the ball of her foot and walked away.

Despite what Micah accused her of, she'd let down her guard, allowed the smile to slip, to show the true emotions that Micah had been telling her all along would have been safe with him.

But it wasn't enough.

Micah drove away, taking her crushed heart with him.

She'd give him space. All the space he needed. But she wasn't going to wait around for him to show back up, because experience had taught her that Micah Holland took his sweet time coming back home. And apparently, she wasn't worth rushing home for.

Paige tightened her coat around her, a sharp chill slithering down the back of her neck. It felt cold enough to snow.

Again.

She was ready for winter to end.

Was it too early to start dreaming about tropical vacations?

Maybe that's what she needed—a vacation, time to get away and think things through. Maybe it would help her gain some perspective.

Before she could even consider that, she had chores to do. Goats needed to be fed and watered. Then she needed to head back to the cottage to get ready for church.

The last thing she wanted was to sit in the sanctuary, which was supposed to be a safe place, and be judged by those around her. To answer questions about last night. To hear the whispers and rumors of her failure.

Maybe she would skip today. She could always catch the service online.

Yesterday had been nearly perfect until that stupid interview.

Fresh tears warmed the backs of her eyes,

but she blinked them away. Tears led to nothing but trouble.

After feeding and watering the goats at the Holland barn, she let them out in the pasture Jake had created for them with movable fencing, then returned inside to scrub her hands in the deep sink. Once she was sure the goats were fine until evening, she headed for her car.

As she drove past Ian's house, the dark windows peered at her like all hope had been extinguished.

Was Micah really gone? If so, what was he going to do with his property? What would it take to bring him home for good?

She couldn't keep asking those questions when she had no idea how to answer them. She needed to put Micah out of her mind.

At least for now.

Right. That was about as possible as living without breathing.

She pulled into the cottage driveway and cut the engine. Instead of getting out, she rested her head against the seat back, closed her eyes and let out a shaky breath.

Why hadn't she just stayed on the porch? She could've let Micah have his space and then he'd come home and they'd work through everything.

But no, that wasn't good enough. She needed

to try and fix it. She had to succeed at getting him to change his mind.

Instead, she failed.

And he drove away without looking back.

She opened her car door and trudged inside the cottage. Scooping up an excited Charlotte, she headed for the kitchen and lit the fire beneath the teakettle.

Maybe a hot cup of tea and a soak in the tub would help with her perspective.

An hour later, she left the bathroom in a billow of steam and her cup empty.

Her heart still felt as heavy.

She tightened the belt to her bathrobe, then finger-combed her hair as she headed to the kitchen to refill her mug.

Someone tapped quietly on her front door. Her heart jumped as she gripped the edge of the counter.

Micah.

She ran her fingers through her hair, wishing now she had taken the time to dry it. She slowed her step so it didn't look like she was hurrying. She opened the door, and the air whooshed out of her chest. "Willow. Hey. Come in."

Her best friend stepped inside, closing the door behind her. "You sound disappointed. Expecting someone else?"

Paige shook her head as her eyes drifted to

her toes. "Expecting, no. Wishing? Yes. I was about to make another cup of tea. Want one?"

"Sure, sounds great."

"What's up?"

"Nat called and told me what happened between Micah and his family."

"Well, you know more than I do, because Micah didn't tell me anything."

While they waited for the water to boil, Willow shared the details of what had happened in the Holland kitchen. "Where is Micah now? Is he okay?"

Paige pulled a mug out of the cabinet for Willow and set it on the counter. She reached for a foil-wrapped tea bag. Her fingers trembled as she tried to tear it open. The teakettle whistled, and Paige poured the water over the tea bag, feeling drained as the weight of the last twenty-four hours pressed on her shoulders. After returning the kettle to the stove and handing the cup to her friend, she leaned against the kitchen sink and wrapped her arms around her waist. "I have no idea where he is. Where he's going. Or what he's going to do. Because the last thing he said was he needed space."

"I'm so sorry. Is there anything I can do?" Willow stirred honey into her tea.

"Other than track him down and shake some sense into him?" Paige laughed, but her tone sounded brittle. She retrieved a plate, filled it with scones Abby and their mother had made, and set it on the table.

"We all know that Micah has his own timetable. You have to remember he's gone through so much over the last several years. But the Micah who's been home for the last couple of months is not the same Micah who popped in from time to time since getting injured. This new Micah was ready to start fresh and put down roots."

"But he didn't stay. I wasn't enough reason to keep him here."

Willow reached for Paige's hand. "You know I love you, right?"

Paige nodded.

"Good, because I don't want you to think I'm taking sides, but did you tell him you would help him through whatever was eating at him?"

Paige rewound her conversation in the driveway with the man who had stolen her heart. Instead of offering sympathy and empathy, she had hurled veiled accusations at him. And cried, making it about her and what she wanted.

She broke apart the scone, but instead of eating it, she crumbled it between her fingers.

"Paige, I know you. And I know how you keep such a tight rein on your emotions. But you have to trust the guy, to know he's going to be there for you. You can't keep walling him out. Be patient with him."

"But that's just it—I didn't want him out this time. I showed how I was feeling, but I couldn't keep it together and now he needs space. How am I supposed to trust him to be there for me if a simple tear sent him running?"

"Well, after talking with Nat, I don't think this was about you but more to do with his reaction to what happened in the kitchen at the farmhouse. Paige, he punched his father. I've been friends with Micah for a long time, and I know he has to be absolutely gutted about it. He lashed out at you because of his own feelings of failure and frustration. Perhaps he needed more space from his family than from you."

"So how long do I wait? Do I try to call him or text him?"

"No, let him come to you. Natalie and Evan are getting married in a few days. I'm sure he'll be home for that. You're just going to have to trust that what you guys had is not lost."

Trust. So easy to say, yet so much harder to do.

But she'd listen to her wise friend, because if her relationship with Micah was meant to be, then he'd come home. And she'd do whatever was necessary to show she'd be there for him.

* * *

Micah should've known Ian would have gotten his own way all the way to the end.

After spending less than ten minutes in Ginny's office, Micah slammed out the door and strode to his SUV. He threw himself behind the wheel and smacked his head against the seat back.

What was he going to do now?

All he wanted was to dissolve the partnership with Paige.

But Ginny had remained firm in maintaining Ian's wishes, reminding him if he chose to walk away, then Paige wouldn't receive the final installment of the money, either. He was even willing to give her his share and everything.

If only they had planned for the open house to take place after they'd signed the final paperwork. Then Micah would have been free to do as he wanted instead of being bound by the ridiculous conditions of Ian's will.

He'd hoped a few days away, to clear his head, to make sense of what had happened, would help him to figure out where to go next.

But he wasn't any closer to an answer.

He turned into his driveway and parked behind the farm truck.

Great.

He stepped out of his vehicle and crossed

to the porch, where his dad sat in one of the Amish-made rocking chairs.

"Dad. What are you doing here?" Micah's eyes skimmed over the purple bruise on his father's lined face.

"We need to talk."

Micah nodded, then opened the front door and held it for him. "How about some coffee?"

"I won't say no to a cup."

In the kitchen, Micah retrieved two mugs from the cabinet, then set one under the Keurig and waited for it to brew. Once it was finished, he handed it to his dad and then made his own cup.

Anything to delay the lecture that was sure to be coming. And the disappointment that lingered between them.

Knowing he couldn't put it off any longer, Micah took a sip of the hot brew, then set it on the counter. "Listen, Dad. I'm sorry. So sorry. There are no words to make up for what I did to you. But I promise the last thing I wanted was to hurt you."

"Micah, that punch was nothing. That's not what hurts the most. You went to Ian instead of me. I guess I've prided myself on being the kind of dad who was always there for his kids. So why him?"

"Ian was easier to face."

"You couldn't face your old man?"

"Dad, I have always been the family screwup. I didn't want to lay on the disappointment. More fuel for Jake."

Dad scowled and brushed away Micah's words. "Forget about your brother. We've all made our share of mistakes. So, what were you planning to do? Run away again, instead of facing your giants?"

Just wanting to clear his head, Micah hadn't looked at it as running away, but his father was the second person to accuse him of that.

He shook his head and dropped his chin to his chest. "No, I wasn't running. Despite what you or Paige may think. I shouldn't have kept my arrest a secret, but it was in the past, and I didn't think it would matter anymore. I guess I was wrong. I just wanted some space to figure out where to go from here."

Dad scratched his forehead, then folded his arms over his chest. "How about trusting God? He doesn't give us big dreams only to take them away."

"I don't know if this is a big dream."

"You want to help others like you, don't you?"

Micah nodded. "Yes, but it's been such a struggle. Is it even worth it?"

"Nothing worth having comes easy. You just have to decide if you're willing to fight for what you want to do with your life…and who you want to spend it with."

"Yeah, that ship's sailed. Paige won't want anything to do with me after the way I hurt her. I even went to Ginny's today to see about dissolving our partnership so Paige could have everything. But Ian made that impossible. Even if I sign everything over to Paige, that violates the agreement and we both lose the final installment of the inheritance. We both need to be there to sign the paperwork in order to get the last installment of our money."

Dad chuckled, shaking his head. "Ian must've expected something like this to happen. Otherwise, he would have just given you the money upon his death. What do you think the lesson is he wants you to learn?"

"I don't know. I just don't know anymore."

His father pulled out a letter from his back pocket and handed it to Micah. "Maybe this will help you gain some perspective."

Frowning, Micah took it from him. He turned it over to see his name in Ian's scrawl. "What's this?"

"Another letter from him. He asked me to give it to you once you and Paige had signed the final paperwork. Even though you haven't done that yet, I think this will help you to make up your mind. Just promise you won't go anywhere without talking to me first." Dad stepped forward and pressed a hand on Micah's shoulder.

If only Micah could be eight years old all over again and hurl himself into his father's arms. If only things could be that simple or solved in such a childlike way. When he was younger, Micah had known there was nothing his father could not fix. But since losing his arm, he'd become aware of how some problems could never be repaired.

"There's nothing your Heavenly Father can't fix, son. Including the problems you're wrestling with right here." His father thumped a knuckle against Micah's chest. "You and Jake need to have a heart-to-heart. Stop blaming each other and start working together as a family. We've had enough heartache over the past several years, and I'm not going to watch my boys tear each other apart any longer. Got that?"

Heat stole across Micah's face as he recalled how going after Jake had ended up hurting his father, his champion, the one who had always been there for him in the past.

"Jake blames me for Mom's death."

"No, I don't," a voice said from the doorway.

Micah's head jerked up. His brothers stood identically in the entry, hands on their hips and feet apart. He hadn't heard the door open. He straightened and shoved a hand in his front pocket. "What are you guys doing here?"

Tuck stepped forward, stretching out hand. "We're here to apologize. We haven't been the best brothers over the last few years, but that doesn't mean we can't start fresh and do better moving forward."

Micah rubbed a hand under his nose, his throat thickening. He lifted his chin and caught Jake's steady gaze. "When you came home after Mom's death and heard what had happened, you blamed me. You said if I had charged my phone like a responsible adult, then Mom wouldn't have needed to come out to the field to find me and let me know about the bad weather."

Jake's face paled. "Micah, I was stupid and angry. You were not at fault for Mom's death. No one could have predicted how quickly that tornado swept over the hill. You got her to the barn. Who knows what could've happened if she hadn't been out in the field? This is not your fault. And honestly, I was dealing with my own mistakes—my failed marriage with Tori the first time around, then my buddy Leo's death. I pushed some of that on you. It was wrong."

"Then why did you call me Micah the Menace yesterday?"

"Apparently stupidity flows well in my veins. I screwed up. I tend to speak before my brain has time to engage. Don't worry—these knuckleheads set me straight." He jerked a thumb over his shoulder at Tucker and Evan leaning in the doorway watching the exchange. "I've given you a hard time because I've seen so much promise in you and you seemed to be throwing it all away. I'm sorry. I really am. I've made mistakes I'm not proud of, but I've learned from them. And I know you have, too."

Evan shoved away from the door and rounded the table to stand in front of Micah. "Dude, we all make mistakes. Look at me—I have a son I didn't know about for five years. My own recklessness caused the demise of my kayaking career. But you know what? After sifting through the ashes of disappointment and learning how to cope with the PTSD that hit after my accident, God has brought redemption. In a few days, I'm marrying the most perfect woman for me, and we'll be together as a family for our son." He stretched out his arms. "And you're home. That's an answer to prayer."

Evan's eyes welled up, and he didn't even wipe away the tear that slid down his tanned cheek. "We need to walk away from the past to embrace what's waiting for us in the future. You've worked so hard over the past couple of months, man, to get this house ready and your program up and running to give someone else the courage to face their future."

"Hey, man. I know what it's like to experience loss." Tucker pressed a hand to his heart. "I lost my beautiful Rayne and had two babies to care for. But I couldn't have done it without family. Life has its struggles, ups and downs that we may not always be ready for, but if you stay the course, then you could have everything you've always wanted, including that pretty occupational therapist who has stolen your heart."

"Paige and I are just friends. And I'm not even sure about that anymore."

Evan laughed, the sound bouncing around the room. "Dude, you are so blind. Sure, you two may be friends, but there is so much more going on. We can all see it. Now you have to decide what you're going to do about it—man up and tell her how you feel or walk away and live with the regret. Walking away may be easier, but digging in to do the hard work will reap the sweetest reward."

Dad edged in front of his brothers and took Micah by his shoulders. He peered into his eyes. "Listen to me and listen good—you're as worthy to be a part of this family as any of us. We're Holland Strong. We may bend, but we won't break. And even in those times of bending, we're here walking beside you, giving you the extra hand when you need it. No one is worthy in God's kingdom, but His grace covers all of us. And He uses all things for the good of His glory. No matter what you've gone through over the past few years, those are in the past. Allow them to refine you and turn you into someone who can give others that necessary hand up. Be someone whose testimony will reflect God's glory."

The pressure in Micah's chest threatened to pry apart his rib cage. He threw himself into his father's arms. His brothers gathered around, encircling him.

He was wrong.

He did have a place in this family, and now he was home, where he belonged. He needed the strength of his family to fight for the next most important thing—recapturing Paige's heart.

Chapter Fifteen

Paige really needed to pull herself together.

With Natalie and Evan's wedding this afternoon, she needed to support her friends, not cast a shadow over their day with her pitiful attitude.

She finished rinsing out the buckets and then refilled them with fresh water. After hanging them in the stalls, she filled the goats' grain buckets and made a mental note to order feed.

The remaining goats needed to be dewormed today. Usually Micah helped her, but she hadn't seen him in a week.

He'd wanted space, so she had given it to him.

And she'd tried not to let that rejection carve out her chest.

Once the goats had gobbled their breakfast, Paige let them out into the makeshift pen—still so grateful to the Hollands for their generosity—then went to work cleaning their stalls and laying down a fresh layer of hay and bedding.

Paige broke apart the last bale, then swiped the back of her wrist across her forehead. Normally she didn't mind the work, but the past week of sleepless nights was taking its toll. She'd get through today, then she could use tomorrow to catch up on much-needed rest.

Tires crunched in the barnyard. Her heart jumped.

Stop it.

Her mother appeared in the open doorway, casting a long shadow across the freshly swept floor.

"Mom, what's wrong? Where's Abby?"

"Nothing's wrong. I just wanted to talk to you. Abby's at home with Grandma and Grandpa getting ready for the wedding." Mom reached into her jacket pocket, pulled out an envelope and handed it to Paige. "I wanted to give this to you."

Paige took the envelope with her name in Ian's messy handwriting. She ran a thumb over the ink. "What's this?"

Mom shrugged. "I don't know. Ian asked me to give it to you when I felt you'd be ready to read it."

Paige shoved it in her back jeans pocket. "I'll read it once I finish these chores."

"You know, Paige, you don't have to do this

on your own. You could always hire someone to give you a hand with the chores, freeing you to spend more time with your therapy work."

"I prefer to do things on my own."

"You've always been so independent."

"Like I had any choice." She winced as the words bounced off the stalls. She hadn't meant to say them out loud.

"What's that supposed to mean?"

"Nothing. Forget it."

Mom moved deeper into the barn and rested a hand on Paige's arm. "Honey, if you're upset about something, talk to me. I'm always here for you."

Paige tightened her fingers around the handle of the broom. Then she dragged her fingers through her hair, spiking her skin with a straight piece of hay. "Actually, Mom, no, I can't. You have your hands full with your job and Abby. There's no room left for me."

Her mother's eyes widened as her mouth dropped open. "What are you talking about? That's so not true. I always have time for you, but you never seemed to need me."

"Because you don't have time. Remember that time after Dad died, and I needed your help with a homework assignment? You told me you didn't have time and I had to figure it out for myself. I'm not mad. I'm not upset. I'm just stating a fact."

"Oh, Paige, I'm so sorry. I don't remember that."

"I do. I started crying because I was so frustrated, and you told me to pull myself together, that I needed to be the strong one." She'd held on to that resentment for so long, carrying unnecessary burdens. But now, confessing it released a sense of relief.

"You are a strong woman, Paige."

"But I don't always want to be the strong one, Mom. Everyone else gets to lose their temper and react, but not me. Keep it together, Paige. Don't lose control, Paige. Otherwise, you'll let others down and drive them away." Paige's voice caught as the words in her head bounced off the barn walls. Pressure pulsed behind her ribs, causing her chest to ache. Her eyes filled, but she blinked back the tears.

Her mother stood silent, her brow creased and her eyes shining. Paige hadn't meant to hurt her.

"Paige, I don't know what to say other than I'm so sorry I made you feel like you couldn't rely on me. Or you had to bottle your emotions. After your dad died, life was… Well, I was suddenly a single mother with a teenager and a toddler with a disability. I didn't do a great job of holding it together. But you can always come to me with anything. I love you."

"I love you, too." Her worry eased at this simple exchange. Of course her mother loved her.

"So what's going on with you and Micah?"

At the sound of his name, the tears that battled for control crashed through the stronghold and escaped down her cheeks. Paige dropped the broom and buried her face in her hands, her shoulders shaking.

Mom wrapped her arms around her and drew her into her embrace.

The pain of the past week released as Paige struggled for control.

"That's it. Let it out." Mom stroked her hair, her soothing voice massaging those tender places in Paige's heart.

Drained and fatigued, Paige pulled away, her chest shuddering as she wiped her eyes with the hem of her long-sleeved T-shirt. "I'm sorry."

"For what? Crying? No need. Tears are healing. You need to be able to let them out to move forward."

"But I broke down in front of Micah last weekend and it drove him away."

Mom reached for Paige's hands. "Honey, I had a long talk with Chuck and Claudia the other day. You didn't drive Micah away. He's wrestling with some of his own issues, namely, trying to figure out who he is. You really care for him, don't you?"

"I love him, Mom. Even when he's being a jerk."

Mom laughed. "Honey, we can all be jerks at times. Show him some grace." She swept an arm over the barn. "This…what you two are doing together…it's going to be beautiful."

"I don't know where I stand with him."

"Micah's a good man. If you want to be a part of his life, then fight for what you want. Show him you're not giving up hope."

"I don't even know where he is right now. What if he doesn't want me?"

"I have a good feeling about you two." Mom pulled a tissue out of her coat pocket and pressed it into Paige's hand. "I need to get back to the house and help Abby, but I wanted to check on you. Don't forget to read Ian's letter." Her mother kissed her cheek, then waved as she headed out the door.

Paige picked up the broom and put away her cleaning supplies. After checking on the goats, she opened the door to her car and climbed in behind the wheel. She pulled the envelope out of her back pocket and slid her finger under the seal. Unfolding the paper, the words blurred as she read, hearing Ian's voice in her head. He mentioned how proud he was of everything she'd accomplished and how he hoped her program grew to a great success.

I know you and Micah have your differences, but you also bring out the best in each other. Be patient with him and show him how much you value your relationship.

Paige held the letter against her chest. *Oh, Ian.* She missed him so much.

Fresh tears warmed her eyes. She allowed them to escape down her cheeks as she backed out of the barnyard. Returning to her cottage to get ready for her best friend's wedding, Paige girded her heart for battle.

If she and Micah were going to have any kind of relationship, then his need for space had to come to an end. How could they come together with so much distance between them?

Micah knew what had to be done. But would it be enough?

He brushed his hand across the back of his bare neck.

All he wanted was to prove to Paige he was a changed man, and he was the right one for her. Now to get through this wedding and show her the beauty of their future.

Not that he wanted to rush his brother's big

day or anything. After all, Evan and Natalie deserved their wedding to be special.

He just wanted to talk to Paige.

He missed her.

After seeing her daily for the past couple of months, being away from her this past week had left a hole in his chest. A hole of his own making. A hole only she could fill.

Now if only he could get her to look at him.

With a smile in place, she glided down the aisle gracefully, wearing a burgundy dress that swept her knees. Her hair had been curled and lay over her shoulder, inviting him to twirl one tress around his finger. Eyes facing forward, she took her place in front of Willow, the co-maid of honor.

The music changed to the processional. The guests stood as Natalie appeared in the doorway on her father's arm, wearing a rose gold gown that hugged her waist and flared in a lacy stream to the floor. Her dark hair had been caught up on the side with a bunch of flowers that matched her bouquet.

Next to him, Evan sucked in a sharp breath, and the look of love on his brother's face gave Micah hope for his own future.

Once Natalie and Evan were joined at the altar, Paige reached for Nat's bouquet.

Her gaze connected with his, and her eyes widened, her fingers hesitating.

The rest of the ceremony passed in a blur. If Micah had been given a pop quiz on what had been said, he would've failed, because he had kept his attention on Paige during the service.

The guests clapped, and behind him, his brothers whistled.

Micah jerked his attention back to the bride and groom to find them kissing.

After they walked back up the aisle as Mr. and Mrs. Evan Holland, Micah moved forward and joined Paige. He leaned close, his lips brushing her ear. "You look gorgeous."

Her lips remained frozen in a tight smile, but the softness in her eyes made him realize hope was not lost.

Once they stepped outside in the February sunshine that warmed the cold air, Paige turned to him, her eyes glistening and a genuine smile curving her lips. She pressed warm palms against his bare cheeks, then ran her fingers over the back of his head. "You shaved. And cut your hair."

He reached for her hand and pressed a kiss against her knuckles. "I did it for you. I know we have a lot going on, but promise me you and I will be able to talk later."

She smiled sweetly. "I would like that."

"Great. I'm going to hold you to that."

After the photographer had corralled the wedding party and families for pictures, they headed to the reception being held at Natalie's parents' home.

After dinner had been served and the cake cut, the DJ invited Evan and Natalie to take the floor for their first dance as husband and wife.

Micah threw back the rest of his punch, set his plastic cup on the table and slid back his chair. He'd been patient enough. Now he wanted nothing more than to hold Paige in his arms.

He'd made it halfway to Paige when his niece, Olivia, dressed in her light pink flower girl dress, stopped in front of him and tugged on his left arm. "Uncle Micah, would you dance with me?"

"Dance?" As he looked into her pleading blue eyes, his refusal stuck in his throat. "I'd love to, Princess."

Micah took her small hand in his as she settled her other hand on his waist, then stepped on his feet. "This is how I dance with Daddy."

He looked over to where Tucker sat next to Isabella, his arm around the back of her chair. He raised his punch glass and grinned.

The song ended, and Micah knelt in front of Olivia and pressed a kiss to her soft cheek. "Thanks for being my dance partner, Livie."

"You're welcome, Uncle Micah." She shot him a toothy smile, then skipped back to the table to climb into Tuck's lap.

Micah straightened and turned, nearly running into Paige. He shot out his arm to keep from plowing into her.

She cupped a hand around his elbow and smiled. "Is your dance card full, or do you have room for one more?"

Micah hesitated a second.

Paige dropped her hand and took a step back. "If you'd rather not…"

He grabbed her hand and pulled her to him. "No, it's not that."

He was botching this.

He cupped his fingers around hers and imagined wrapping his other arm around her waist.

Her hand settled on his waist. Her scents of citrus and mint wreathed around them.

"Actually, other than dancing with Livie just now, you were the last person I danced with."

"At our high school prom. With that cheesy 'Under a Starry Night' theme."

"You wore a yellow gown with those skinny rhinestone straps and layers of fluff that looked like cake frosting."

She laughed, the sound spearing his heart. "You are such a guy. I loved that dress. I felt like a princess on the arm of a handsome prince."

"And now you're on the arm of the beast." He laughed as he spoke the words, but she didn't join in.

"Is that how you still see yourself?" The light in her eyes was replaced with a seriousness that left him feeling a little exposed.

"Come on, Paige. I was joking."

Maybe.

"Were you?"

"Despite the cheesy theme, that was a fun night."

"Remember when we competed in the kite-flying festival a couple of years later. You promised to take me to a movie if I beat you. But then you left town without paying up."

"I know, and I'm sorry. I promise to make it up to you, even if it's nearly a decade later. The tornado did more that destroy the farm and kill Mom. Our family fell apart."

She slid her hand away from his waist and cupped his cheek. "I know it's been devastating, but look at you guys now." She waved a hand across the room. "You're all picking up those broken pieces and restoring your lives, making them even better and stronger than before."

Micah's eyes skimmed over the couples on the dance floor, bouncing from his dad dancing with Claudia, Jake dancing with Tori, Tucker and Isabella, and finally Evan folding his new bride in his protective embrace as if he planned never to let her go.

Yes, his family had done an amazing job of putting the pieces of their lives back together.

Now it was his turn.

The song ended. Paige stepped back, but Micah didn't let go of her hand. "Come on. Let's go for a walk."

After retrieving their coats, Micah led her outside where moonlight streamed across the frozen ground. A chilly wind whisked over them as they walked past Natalie's parents' house and onto the snow-covered dirt road that led them away from the celebration.

Once they were out of sight from the Bishop property, Micah stopped in the middle of the road and released Paige's hand. He cupped her face and caressed her silky skin with his thumb. "I'm sorry, Paige, for everything. I'm sorry for not telling you about my arrest. I was too ashamed. Not once did I think about the impact it would have on your business."

"It's in the past, Micah. Anyone who knows you well knows you're not that same person anymore."

"Maybe not, but you were right—I was trying to hide my scars. But they are a part of who I am and what I've been through."

She trailed her fingers down the healed wounds

on his face. "We all have scars. Yours are more visible, but they're also healed. I'm proud of who you are, Micah. You have a kind, tender heart, and your desire to help others to live their best lives is inspiring. I'm not talking about the challenges you've overcome, but also your character."

He tapped her gently on the nose. "You inspire me. You turn children's 'can'ts' into 'cans.' And you do the same for me."

"What is this? Some sort of mutual admiration society?"

He reached into his pocket and pulled out a royal blue velvet bag. He worked the opening with his thumb and forefinger, letting the bag flutter to the ground. He hooked the silver chain around his finger and held it in front of her.

Paige gasped. Her eyes widened as she reached slowly for the dangling heart that glinted in the moonlight. "My necklace. Where did you find it?"

"I knew how much it meant to you. After you left, I sifted through the compost for you. I was just about to give up when I found it. It's not the original chain, but if you want that one, we can get it repaired and cleaned." He touched the hearts dangling at the end of the chain. "I added another heart. It's a little bigger, but that's to show how the love from your past can grow into your future if you're willing to give it a chance."

"It's beautiful. Thank you, Micah. Two little words seem so insignificant, but I don't know what else to say." She looked up at him, her eyes shining.

"How about adding three more words?" Micah cupped her face once again and took a step closer. "I love you, Paige. I love the way you challenge me. I love your compassion. I love the way your nose turns red when you're holding back tears. But, most of all, you see past my scars to who I am…a stubborn prodigal who needed a strong woman to show him the way home."

Paige curled her fingers around his. "At first, I resented Ian for throwing us together in that ridiculous partnership, but now I see it as one of the wisest decisions he could have made. Micah, I want to be more than partners in business— I want to partner with you in life, through the good and the bad."

"Will you trust me with your heart as long as I promise not to break it? I love you, and I want to spend the rest of our lives showing you."

The words Paige longed to hear spilled over Micah's lips like a love song.

The vulnerability in his eyes as he waited for her response glued back together some of the broken pieces in her heart—pieces only he could put together.

But only if she claimed his promises.

She opened her hand and looked at the delicate silver filigree chain draped over her palm. She traced both hearts—one she'd worn for nearly two decades holding on to the past and the other that offered her a promising future with the one man who had forced his way past her mask and wanted to know the true her.

With her vision blurring, Paige unhooked the chain, then removed the smaller heart. She crouched and picked the velvet bag off the ground, slid the heart inside, reached for Micah's hand and pressed it into his palm, curling his fingers around it. "Losing this necklace broke me. Not only for what it represented, but also the way you allowed me to cry over the loss. But you searched through the muck and mire to find it."

"And I'd do it all over again, Paige."

She pressed her lips over his knuckles. "I know you would. I know it's not that much of a grand gesture, but I want you to have my heart—the token tied to my happiest memory with the man who loved me unconditionally. The man who kept me safe. The man who encouraged me not to settle. Because I haven't. For the first thirteen years of my life, he was the keeper of my heart. Now you hold that responsibility. I love you, Micah. I trust you with my whole heart and promise to show you nothing but complete authenticity. I want to partner with you to see where life…and love take us."

Micah slipped the heart she had given him into his shirt pocket and patted it. "I will always keep your heart safe."

Then he lowered his head and claimed her lips, sealing his promises. He pressed his forehead against hers. "Marry me, Paige. I don't have a ring. In fact, I didn't even expect to propose, because, quite frankly, I didn't know if you wanted to see me again. But this feels right. If you want to wait, I understand."

Paige slid her arms around his neck. "I don't want to wait. And I don't need a ring." She clutched the heart hanging from her neck. "You gave me your heart. That's all I want. Yes, Micah, I will marry you. Thank you for having the courage to come back home."

Micah pulled her into his embrace and tightened his arm around her. He dropped a kiss on top of her head. "I will always come home to you."

That was a promise she'd trust him to keep.

Epilogue

Chuck Holland couldn't be a happier man.

It had taken some years and some time on his knees, but God had answered his prayers and brought his wayward children home.

And now their family had grown to include four daughters-in-law, who had become the perfect spouses for his sons, and four grandchildren…and hopefully, counting.

Chuck tightened his hold on his glass of celebratory sparkling grape juice and allowed his gaze to roam over his family standing together in front of Ian's place, which had been renovated according to Micah and Paige's vision.

Jake, Tori and baby Charlie. Tucker, Isabella, Olivia and Landon. Evan, Natalie and Aidan. And now Micah and Paige, newly wedded, who had returned home from their brief honeymoon last night to get ready for today's grand opening ceremony.

An unseasonably warm March breeze toyed with the wide yellow ribbon wrapped around the pillars on the front porch of Ian's renovated home.

Not that Chuck was complaining.

It had been a harsh winter.

But spring came after the thaw and offered new growth.

Growth he'd been blessed to see in his family.

"A man doesn't live to be my age without learning some life lessons or living with regrets. But the one thing I will never regret is my family. Or what we've gone through. Each one of those defining moments have brought us to the feet of our Heavenly Father." Chuck stretched a hand out to his beautiful wife, Claudia, who understood that deep stab of grief after losing her first husband. "When that tornado nearly wiped out the farm and took my sweet Lilly, I didn't know how we'd survive, but God had a plan. He put important people in our lives to help us to find hope in the heartache."

"Hear! Hear!" His sons raised their glasses in unison while keeping their eyes on their spouses.

"As we gather here to celebrate the grand opening of A Hand Up House, let's pray for the men coming to live in this home. May they be walking toward a better future. May they hold on to hope no matter what storms come their way. And may God continue to bless Micah and Paige as they start their new life together and help others do the same."

Hand in hand, Micah and Paige picked up the pair of scissors lying on the wheelchair ramp coming off the side of the porch and rounded the front of the house to cut the ribbon in half.

Micah let out a whoop, fist pumped the air, then wrapped his arm around his beautiful bride and kissed her. "We did it, babe."

She slipped her arms around his neck. "You did it. Your vision."

"I couldn't have done it without you, Mrs. Holland." He pressed his forehead against hers.

"Oh, I love how that rolls right off your tongue."

Chuck resisted an eye roll and cleared his throat.

The newlyweds broke apart, and pink colored Paige's cheeks.

Chuck stuck his left hand out to Micah, his voice feeling a little gruff. "I'm so proud of you, Micah, and I know your mother is, too."

Micah pulled him in for a hug. "Thanks, Pops. And thanks for never giving up on me."

"I knew you'd return. It was just a matter of time."

"Yes, my road to redemption may have been filled with twists, detours and a few potholes along the way, but the ultimate destination led me to one place—home."

Right where he belonged.

* * * * *

Dear Reader,

When I started the Holland Brothers series, inspired by childhood memories on my grandparents' dairy farm, I had no idea the journey God would take me through the writing of each of the brothers' stories. But that's so like God, isn't it? He uses His goodness and grace to refine our lives so we can reflect His glory...and learn those unexpected lessons.

When I introduced Micah in *Season of Hope*, I didn't know his story until I started plotting it. But I knew the somewhat prodigal son needed to come home for his story to be told.

And that's how it is for each one of us—we are prodigal children, standing outside the center of God's will, and He's waiting for each of us to come home to Him. His amazing grace will redeem us so He can lead us to tell our stories that reflect His grace and glory.

It's not easy, but when we love and trust Him, He works all things (even the broken parts of our lives) for good.

Finding hope in the heartache has been the theme for this series, but I feel it's a promise we can hold on to through every season in our lives.

I hope you enjoyed Micah and Paige's story—a story that took them down a road of needing to trust God…and each other…to tell their stories and to be used for His divine purpose.

I value you, my readers, and I love to hear from you. Visit me at lisajordanbooks.com and feel free to email me at lisa@lisajordanbooks.com.

Embracing His grace,
Lisa Jordan

HARLEQUIN SELECTS COLLECTION

19 FREE BOOKS IN ALL!

From Robyn Carr to RaeAnne Thayne to Linda Lael Miller and Sherryl Woods we promise (actually, GUARANTEE!) each author in the Harlequin Selects collection has seen their name on the *New York Times* or *USA TODAY* bestseller lists!